Double Delight

Julie Castle

Warning: Not intended for persons under the age of 18. May contain coarse language and mature content that may disturb some readers. Reader discretion advised.

Cover Art Design by: Kelly Moran/Rowan Prose Publishing
Photo Credit: Adobe Images
First Printing
ISBN: 978-1-961967-33-5
Rowan Prose Publishing, LLC
www.RowanProsePublishing.com

Published in the United States of America

Double Delight (series) Reviews

"APRIL LOVE is a romantic and sensual love story. [Castle]
has written a lovely book with two characters who are not only
believable, but that are special individuals."
-Fallen Angel Reviews, 5 stars

"If you are looking for a story with endearing characters, hot sex,
and a HEA ending, pick up APRIL LOVE."
-Enchanted In Romance

"[Castle] writes a book that will keep you up until all hours of
the night. This book is so hot, you will need ice water to cool
down. It's a keeper."
-Coffee Time Romance, 5 cups

"A charming tale sure to capture your heart. This is a book
definitely well worth reading."
-Romance Junkies

"MONICA'S MANHUNT is beautifully intense."
-The Romance Studio

APRIL LOVE

Julie Castle

CHAPTER 1

I desperately need to get laid, April Brooks decided, climbing onto a barstool in the back booth at Red's Bar & Grill. Resting my evening sandal-shod feet on the table's brass rail, I surveyed the dancing couples with an envious eye. It should have been easy back in my sleepy hometown, but it wasn't. I didn't want permanence, just a real man to finally make me feel like a real woman.

Was that too much to ask?

Apparently, the universe said yes, I realized, letting out a sigh. Men might be cheating dogs in general, but they did have their uses, like ridding a twenty-eight-year-old woman of her virginity. I wanted to find out what I was missing. Ached to, actually—if those hollow longings between my legs were anything to go by. I needed a dream lover—for one night.

Smoothing my new blue dress out on my lap, I figured it definitely beat my usual garb of lab coats and business suits. They belonged to the old me, the ex-dowdy assistant college professor. This sexy new dress fit the me I wanted to become. I was determined to reinvent myself as the owner of a successful Bed & Breakfast, and as a woman with at least some semblance of a sex life.

The jukebox twanged a song about 'friends in low places.' That about summed up Red's, and it fit my mood. I hadn't been able to resist coming here after leaving a friend's wedding reception, needing a distraction. Twin calamities had flattened me like a one-two punch two weeks ago, and I was still trying to get over them. First, my Aunt Sadie had been incapacitated with a stroke. A week later, my personal life and career had imploded when I walked in on my fiancé and mentor, Edmund Jones, having sex with one of his grad students.

Humiliated, I'd instantly realized our three-year platonic relationship had been nothing but a sham to him. It was a shock to realize what a fool I'd been. For three years, I'd been tamping down my sexual desires, saving myself for a man that didn't even want me. I'd coddled him, supported him, and helped him with his work. In short, I'd been more of a servant than a girlfriend. Edmund had even claimed to suffer from writer's block, and I helped him get published. The truth was, I'd written the articles because he was too lazy, and he'd claimed all the credit. I hadn't minded at the time, feeling like we were a team, and besides, he needed it for tenure.

Walking in on him, his trousers around his ankles and Tiffany kneeling in front of him, her lips swallowing his small red penis as he made disgusting grunting sounds, had vividly taught me how stupid I'd been. I'd resigned my position rather than work under the man anymore.

Moving back home to run The Rosebud had been another move in the right direction, but in some ways, it had only made me feel more discontent with my lot in life. I didn't fit in here, either. Seeing my old high school friends paired off reminded me that life was quickly passing me by. Which explained my showing up at Red's tonight more demoralized than ever. When my best friend Ellen joked that I was so uptight I squeaked, I knew it was painfully true. It was high time I shed my cursed virginity. I needed a dream lover—for one night—to make me feel whole.

Of course, he'd need to be good at sex. That was a given. I definitely required a man who could perform.

Eyeing the selection of guys present, I suddenly had an epiphany. Given my academic background, it would be easiest to approach my deflowering as a research project. I could do this. The perfect candidate's qualifications were quite simple and easy to define. He had to be reasonably good looking. No drop dead gorgeous men need apply, but he did need to be able to wake my slumbering hormones. He had to be very good at sex. And most of all, he couldn't be clingy! After the way Edmund had wailed and pursued me after I'd left him, I couldn't handle clingy. This would amount to a one-time occurrence, so

I wouldn't run the risk of getting attached to him and getting my heart broken.

A burst of masculine laughter from the head of the bar snagged my attention, sending a little fission of heat up my spine. Good God! I recognized that rugged laugh, that powerful stance. Viewing him from the back, I still knew him by heart. And why not? I'd had a huge crush on him as a kid.

Billy Shepard!

Another visceral thrill shot through me. Five years older and the town's rebel without a cause, he still looked good enough to eat. Not classically handsome, no. He was tall, muscular, dangerous, and something about him made me shiver right down to my toes.

Now, Billy Shepard undoubtedly knew how to do it, and I'd bet my bottom dollar he could perform like a super stud. My gaze swept up his long jean clad legs, to focus on his sexy tight butt for a long beat. Biting my lip, I slowly let my gaze drift up his muscular frame to focus on his wavy, coal black hair. Still a bit too long to be considered proper, it brushed his collar. I itched to run my fingers through it. If his front looked half as good as I remembered, I'd just found my man.

My father would have said he was a renegade, my mother would have referred to him as too wild for his own good. I thought he was just plain yummy.

He turned, and my heart fluttered, slamming against my chest. He was still sexy as sin, and twice as good looking. As if he'd felt my stare, he looked straight at me. He'd grown into a hard-edged, handsome man, I conceded. His eyes a dark midnight blue, his nose straight, and his chin strong. Billy's mouth—oh my, his mouth, conjured up all kinds of forbidden fantasies inside me. I wanted to taste it.

"Perfect," I whispered, and he grinned, like he'd read my lips. I looked away, flustered as my body burned.

Will Shepard stood stock still at the bar. The only thing moving was his cock, swelling behind the fly of his jeans. Little April Brooks was giving him a hard-on from across the room. Not so little anymore, he amended. She was nicely filled out, from her sweetly rounded ass to her full breasts, enhanced by the silky dress she wore. They were more than a handful for him, and he had big hands. He'd noticed her the moment she'd entered, tracking her movement across the bar. She was a lethal combination. Half the men in the joint sat up and took notice.

He knew precisely why she was back in sleepy Landis Falls. She was the new proprietress of The Rosebud, one of his firm's biggest construction jobs. He'd been in the midst of the renovation when Sadie Brooks had a stroke two weeks back. Now little April Brooks was back to take the helm. Watching the telltale blush on her face, he figured he had something else he'd like her to take hold of—all twelve inches.

Everything about her was a turn-on, from her red hair to her sparkling green eyes. She was unforgettable. When she was five, he'd chased her with worms and playfully pelted her with snowballs. When she was twelve, she'd been a gangly girl with pigtails, playing the flute in the middle school band. He'd been just off to the Army when she'd been in high school. He remembered the shy former nerd she used to be.

Funny, but he hadn't thought about her for years. He watched her nibble her full lower lip as she peeked back at him, and he groaned. He knew when a woman wanted him. Yeah, he had plans for those luscious lips.

Stalking her way, he acknowledged to himself he was acting like a damned fool, but it didn't slow his stride. He was respectable now. A businessman. His well-respected construction company belonged to the Chamber Of Commerce, for Pete's sake. After his divorce two years back, he'd been very cautious about the women he chose to bed.

But, damn, like a moth drawn to an irresistible flame, he made his way to her side.

I watched Billy cross the floor, his eyes never leaving mine. What now? Considering how busy academic life had kept me, I hadn't learned how to flirt well. And then, he was there, sidling up to me, and I stopped thinking.

Breathing in the mingled scents of sandalwood and man, my heart fluttered again. He seemed to take up the entire space, the noise and people around us receding into insignificance.

He leaned in close. "Hello, pretty lady."

Pretty? Me? Probably just pick-up lines, I decided and promptly got lost in his deep blue eyes. "Hi. I'm...um...Andrea. Yeah, Andrea Bates." This would be easier for me to do if I remained a mystery woman. Like an actress playing a role, I could act sexy if I put my mind to it. I held out my hand for him to shake, watching his reaction to my blatant lie. There was a small twitch of his manly lips as he broke into a friendly smile.

"Will Shepard," he said, setting his beer bottle on the table to shake my hand.

I felt a surge of excitement as his big hand enfolded mine. My gaze darted to the big bulge in his pants, obvious behind the placket of his tight jeans, and I gulped. He was definitely the right choice. Face heating, I looked up, giving him what I hoped was a confidant smile. After a long moment, he let go of my hand and picked up his beer. His thick fingers curled around the long neck bottle.

They were big and rough from manual labor. How would they feel on my sensitive nipples, on the hot spot between my legs that was growing heavy and dewy as I stared at his hand? Tracking my gaze back to his face, I watched him take a sip of his beer, his throat opening and closing as he swallowed.

Unable to hold it in any longer I blurted, "Will Shepard, would you like to take me to bed?"

As my words registered, he choked on his beer for a minute. His eyes flashed, his mouth twitched again, and the bulge in his pants grew bigger.

Yes! I'd made the right choice.

He edged nearer, his crotch bumping my hip. "You don't beat around the bush, do you...ah, Andrea?" he asked with a grin.

Burning where he touched me, I looked up at him, studying the slight flush on his face. He was just as affected by the contact. It was a balm to my wounded femininity.

"I believe in being direct. Well?"

"Sure," he said, his voice a husky bedroom rumble. "I'd love to take you to bed, precious."

The pet name sounded nice, it flowed over me like honey and made my nipples tighten. The space between my legs melted. "Good."

Snatching my purse, I nudged him, getting him to move back so I could slip out of the booth. I'd be cool and sophisticated about this if it killed me. Resisting the urge to grab him by the hand and drag him out of there, I headed for the door. I could hardly believe my beginner's luck. I'd caught big game—Billy Shepard.

He fell into step beside me, possessively looping a long arm around my waist. A sensual shiver shot through me. He must have felt my tremor, because he squeezed, and the breath caught in my throat as my knees wobbled.

When we stepped into the warm June night, I breathed in a lungful of steamy air, collecting my thoughts. The sultry night air stirred my senses, but not as much as the hunk clinging possessively to my waist, as if he didn't want to let me get away. He didn't need to worry, I wasn't going anywhere but the nearest motel. Phase one of my deflowering was about to begin.

Gazing up at him, I couldn't help focusing on his sensual mouth. What would it taste like, feel like, skimming along my tender skin? I stopped by my car and turned to him. "William, if you'd like to follow me to the nearest motel, I'll secure us a room."

His mouth twitched again, as if he thought my offer amusing, and I wondered if I'd made a big mistake. If he wasn't going to take this seriously—

He stepped closer, pressing me back against my car, his eyes twinkling. "Why me, precious? Why'd I get to be the lucky guy?"

He sounded hesitant, and I decided he looked a little concerned.

"Because you're perfect," I said, meaning every word. I watched his mood lighten, his eyes twinkle, and breathed a sigh of relief.

"I'm glad you think so."

"I do."

"Well then," he said, pressing closer. "First of all, only my mother calls me William. How about Will or even Billy, if you like. Second, we'll go to my place, precious."

Sensually overcome as he brushed against me, hot and demanding, I tried to focus on my objections. If I picked the place,

I had the power. But would a macho guy like this go along with being controlled? Would it hurt his male ego for me to pay for the room? Feeling the hard length of his manhood bump against my abdomen, I gasped.

"I don't know, Will."

His smile tightened, leaning into me, my breasts pillowed against his chest. His hands skimmed up my sides, coming to rest on either side of my breasts, his thumbs teasing, inches from my nipples.

A needy moan poured from my mouth as I arched into him, my head falling back.

"I love that sound, red." Taking advantage of my open throat, he bent to nuzzle it, moving to nip at my earlobe.

Swamped by erotic sensation, I could only whimper and press closer.

Sucking on my earlobe he murmured, "Precious, as the one who was asked, I should get to pick the place. It's common sexual courtesy."

Was he teasing me? Pulling back, I missed the pressure of his hot body against my sensitive breasts. Licking my lips, I focused on that sexy mouth of his. "It is?"

"Sure." He grinned at me, his pelvis rocking teasingly against mine.

Sparks of pleasure shot though me. At his wolfish smile, I wondered how many women he'd bedded, and thought about chickening out. "Well, I'm not..."

He cocked his head, watching me. "If you're wondering, I haven't been with a woman for over six months." He smiled, rocking against me again. "As you can feel, I'm primed and ready."

"And not clingy," I added.

He chuckled. "You got that right, precious! I'm definitely not clingy." He backed off, motioned to an old pickup a few slots down. "Hop in the old truckster, and we'll be on our way."

"I'll follow you in my car." I didn't like his domineering tendencies, but I could put up with them for one night. The compensations were obvious—I slanted another look at the bulge in his pants, the spot between my legs hot. I missed the feel of him pressing against me.

"Just remember, Will, I picked you. I'm in charge."

CHAPTER 2

Will glanced at the speedometer and realized he was doing eighty. He eased his foot off the accelerator, telling himself to get a grip. Just because April had asked him to fuck her, it was no reason to freak out. Still, he couldn't help gazing at her headlights in his rearview mirror. Her silver Audi kept pace with his truck. He felt like a kid on Christmas morning. He couldn't wait to unwrap her and sink his dick into her body.

Why was she trying to go incognito? As if he wouldn't recognize her. She might not be the same little nerd she'd been in grade school, but the fire in her green eyes shone just as bright. Back then, he'd noticed her in the same offhanded way he'd notice a real pest. He sure as hell was noticing her now—every luscious curve. He shifted in his seat, his cock swelling.

Picking up men was new to her. He could tell by her guilty blush. Good gravy—a woman who could blush while she asked you to screw her. It boggled his mind, and threatened to drive him right over the edge. Just brushing up against her as she trembled, looking at him like he was a hero sandwich and she was starving, was enough to make him cum in his jeans. But he didn't want to spill it, he wanted to feed her his cock and feel her tremble all over him. The fit would be perfect, he knew. She would be hot, creamy, and ready for him.

Speeding toward his cabin, he decided to ignore all her crap about not being clingy. She was gun-shy for some reason, probably some jerk who'd hurt her. April would soon find out he wasn't that kind of guy. He'd stick like glue until he learned every sultry curve of her body. He also intended to figure out why she was picking up men in bars. Lucky for her, she'd picked him instead of some shark at Red's. As if he'd have allowed anyone else to be in his place.

My hands were damp on the steering wheel, my whole body trembling like something momentous was about to occur. It was just a little harmless sex. People did it every day. I just didn't happen to be one of them. Will was going to remedy that situation for me.

How would it be? What did he look like under those jeans? I'd felt his stiff length as he pressed against me, and it had seemed enormous. My womanhood quivered, growing wet, when I thought about it.

Would I be able to take him? Would he give me enormous pleasure? Just brushing against him had been mind-blowing. What would it be like to have him naked, over me, inside me? The questions replayed in my mind.

Will turned onto a rural lane that snaked around Loon Lake, and I eased my foot off the accelerator, panicking. The Rosebud was across the lake. I could almost see the decrepit Victorian inn I was about to take over from here. Did I want to do this so close to home? What if Will figured out my deception? I didn't like to think of crossing him, not that I'd ever heard of him hitting a woman. A few guys, yeah, but a woman? No. He'd probably just dump me or maybe turn me over his knee. Even that sounded sexy, kinky as it was. I was rapidly turning into one big erogenous zone.

Pressing my foot on the accelerator, I decided to risk it, even if going a little too close to home made me nervous. The Rosebud loomed dark across the water. It'd been shut down for months, undergoing renovations. They'd halted when Sadie had been hospitalized. Now, she was recovering in a rehab center. I was about to resume the renovations. That is, if I could come to an understanding with Ace Contractors. They'd yet to answer any of my messages.

Trailing Will's old truck, I turned into his long driveway. We drove up to a new two-story log cabin. Gazing at the rough-hewn logs in admiration, I decided it was pretty. Sturdy, traditional, just like Will. I had a feeling he'd built it himself, carving out a cozy retreat in the country.

His truck came to a halt. I pulled in next to him as he got out.

This was it. Could I actually bring myself to go through with it, or would I chicken out?

My lips tingled as I gazed at him in the moonlight. His ground-eating stride was closing in on my car.

Too eager for his kisses to be cautious, and playing it cool, I opened my car door. When he reached in to take my hand and help me out of the car, I was touched by his gallantry, and also more than a bit flustered. His warm hand closed over my upper arm as I stood, and he tugged me aside, shutting my car door with a firm clunk. I gave a delighted shiver.

He was so self-assured—masterful, even. Did I want that? I'd wanted to call all the shots, make all the moves. Now, it seemed more exciting to have him do it.

He reached out to touch my cheek, his gaze watchful and hot.

Tender, his soft caress of my cheek made my breath leave me in a heated whoosh.

Clearly puzzled, he asked. "What's wrong, precious?"

"Wrong?" I bit my lip, trying not to look nervous. This was going all wrong. I wanted to appear confident.

He nodded. "You seem uneasy about something."

"Who? Me?" My self-assurance was fading fast, but I was determined to see this through.

Studying me, he drew in a deep breath. "I'll tell you what. Why don't we start things out slow?" His tender tone silenced my lingering doubts.

Slow sounded right to me. I could do slow. "Okay."

He smiled. "How about we try a kiss first?"

Closing my eyes, I pursed my lips and leaned forward, waiting. When nothing happened, I opened my eyes to find him gazing at me.

"Well?"

His eyes narrowed as he frowned. "Haven't you ever been kissed before?"

"Of course, I have!" I insisted, my cheeks flaming. I'd been kissed three times by Edmund—polite little pecks I now knew meant nothing to him. Still, I couldn't quite bring myself to reveal those failures.

"Well, those guys must have been complete amateurs," he muttered. He leaned back against my car and tugged me around to stand in front of him. "Now, lean forward and brush my mouth with yours. Try to make me kiss you back."

Embarrassed and excited, I leaned forward, brushing his firm lips with mine, whisper soft. I let out a sigh. It was nice. But he wasn't kissing me back. I inched closer, stepping between his open feet, and tried again. Pressing my lips against his, I felt his mouth warm and soften. I flicked out my tongue to taste him.

He groaned low in his throat, and I shivered with raw excitement.

His arms went around my neck as I kissed him harder. His mouth opened for me, and my tongue darted inside. It was so exciting. I shuddered, clinging to him. He tasted wonderful, of beer and passion. His mouth molded against mine. I sagged against his strong body, the bulge of his manhood pressing against the juncture of my thighs. My core nestled against him, tingling as he pulled me tight.

I pressed closer to him. Will was kissing me, his tongue slipping into my mouth. His erection pressed hard against me. Whimpering, I all but melted into him, hot all over as my lower body burned.

Now I knew what everyone was raving about. Kissing was wonderful.

My nipples tingled, budded against the solid wall of his chest. I couldn't resist rubbing them against him, the hussies, and gasped at the electric sensation. My panties were getting damp, growing embarrassingly soaked with my wetness as the tingling between my legs increased. I arched my pelvis. His big hands cupped my bottom as he pulled me in, bumping against me.

I whimpered into his mouth as I seemed to have some sort of seizure, my womb contracting, pulsing. Lightning shot through me and I could hardly breathe.

Will held me close, his big hand smoothing my back. Letting him take my weight, I sagged against him. Laying my head against his chest, I listened to his heart race. I could feel it, hear it. And his bulge remained huge. I felt it pressing hard against my rippling femininity, still quivering with little after spasms.

Resting against him, replete, I confessed, "I never knew…"

His hands tightened on my hips. "Don't tell me that was your first."

"First?"

"Orgasm," he said, tightly.

"Oh." My face was hot with a blush, but what the heck? I'd already as good as admitted it. "Yup. My very first."

"Hmm," he rumbled. "You are a mystery."

"Good," I said with a smile, leaning, cuddled against him. A mystery was exactly what I wanted to be to him.

Pushing me back on my heels, he said, "Let's take this inside, precious."

I took his strong hand in mine, wondering what other pleasures I might discover. This first foray into passion was beyond anything I'd imagined. I'd definitely picked the right partner. Will, my instructor in the Art of Love.

He led me toward the dark porch. A big animal's shape suddenly loomed, moving quickly on the porch, frightening me for a moment until I realized it was a hound of some sort.

"Looks like we've got a reception committee."

Tugging her forward, he smiled. "Meet Buck, my dog."

Gazing at the huge shaggy beast as we stepped closer, I couldn't help but be amused. The hound had pointy ears, a burly body, and lots of fur. "That's a dog?"

"Sure," he said, leading me forward. "Best watch dog in town. But don't worry, I promise you, he won't bite." He chuckled, adding, "And neither will I."

"Some watchdog," I said with a smile, seeing the sleepy looking huge mutt clearly as we stepped onto the wraparound wooden porch.

"Buck believes in expending his energy only on important things, just like his master." He scratched Buck's scraggly head. "Right, boy?"

Buck's tail flopped on the floorboards twice, then he lay down and went back to sleep.

"So, you and Buck share a similar work ethic?" I asked, amused as Will opened the cabin's front door.

"You bet." He smiled at her, one raven dark brow quirking. "I'm willing to expend all the energy it takes—on the right projects."

"Such as?" I asked, fascinated as I stepped forward.

"You, sweetheart." He backed me over the threshold. "You are number one on my 'to do' list."

Delighted, I shivered, slightly shocked by the double entendre. He meant to do me, and do me right. I stepped into the house, blushing, as he shut the door. He shot home the lock, and I shivered again, excited and a bit scared. I was in his home, and in his hands. What would he do with me?

He came forward, and I closed my eyes, bracing myself for the sensual onslaught. Would he pounce?

His hand cupped my cheek, his touch soft and gentle, but nothing happened. I opened my eyes. Wasn't he going to kiss me? I craved his kisses now. He looked at me funny, as if he was trying to figure out my secrets.

"You haven't had much experience, have you?"

Did it show that much? I blinked back tears at his tender tone, telling myself they were from frustration.

"No," I admitted, embarrassed. I stared at his sensual mouth. If only he'd kiss me.

He frowned. "If you want to change your mind, leave now."

I shivered, hearing his suddenly gritty tone. He was serious. Not a boy to be played with. But then, I'd never played with boys. This was a special night, and I wasn't about to pass it up. I was determined to learn all the love lessons I'd missed out on.

"I'm not going to change my mind, Will."

"Good. Upstairs." He took my hand, leading me up the open log staircase to a loft bedroom.

When he switched on the light, I glanced around the master bedroom. It was bright and airy, with windows overlooking the lake. I could make out the outline of The Rosebud across the water.

Then I looked at the king-sized bed, covered in a patchwork quilt, and felt a heat wave surge through me. Embarrassed, I hoped he wouldn't notice.

He shut the door and walked over to me. I stood still, not quite knowing what to do with my hands. But his sinful smile made me forget my fear. I reached up to circle his neck with my arms, pulling him down for a kiss. This I knew how to do properly, thanks to him.

Will groaned, legs spread, pulling her tighter against him. She was driving him crazy. Her kisses were enough to make him cum in his jeans. He ground against her, grabbing her generously curved ass, tugging her to him so she could feel how hard he was. She seemed to freeze for a moment before going all fluid on him.

He told himself to take it easy, not scare her. She was a delicate flower to be approached carefully.

He let go of her bottom, hearing her murmur of disappointment. "All in good time, precious," he said, reaching behind her to unzip her dress. She gasped, no doubt embarrassed as he undressed her. After slipping the dress down her body, he let it fall to the floor with a swish. He actually felt her shiver as she leaned against him. "Easy, precious."

He was in a hurry now—desperate for her—but not wanting to scare her. *Delicate flower*, he kept repeating in his head. She wore a prim white set of panties and bra. He still thought she looked sexier than any Victoria's Secret model. His gaze fixed on her full breasts, the nipples poking against the white cotton bra. The embarrassment on her pretty face made him fear she was backing out.

"Undress me," he said to distract her.

She gulped, her blush deepening as she reached up to unbutton his shirt, then he tugged it out of his jeans.

He grinned, pleased he'd taken her mind off her near nudity and put it on him instead. Kicking off his shoes, he waited. She approached his jeans tentatively, unbuckling his belt, and removing it. Then, she unsnapped his jeans and lowered the zipper. He watched her nibble her sexy lower lip as she tugged his jeans, and he thought he'd lose it then and there.

She was so shy. He could almost swear she was a virgin. But would a virgin try to pick up a man? He stepped out of his pants. She was on her knees, blowjob level, but that pleasure could come later. Later, after he'd taken the edge off his need.

Kneeling before him, she pulled down his briefs part way, looking like a virgin sacrifice. He bit back a groan as she studied him in pure fascination. She reached out to brush the throbbing head of his cock with trembling fingers, sliding a curious look up at him.

Taking her hand, he tugged her to her feet. "Bed," was all he could get out, all but tossing her onto it.

She scrambled around to the headboard, eyes wide as saucers. Her gaze focused on his cock as he stripped off his briefs the rest of the way and came toward her. He settled into the bed beside her, reaching for her, kissing her, pressing her back into the mattress. Her arms came around him, holding him tight.

He kissed her, feeling her sweet mouth open for him. His tongue surged inside, tasting her, mastering her. She was sweet. He reached behind her, unhooking her bra.

She stiffened, and he pulled back, looking at her. She was blushing again. Silently, he waited for her protest. When she voiced no objections, he breathed a sigh of relief.

As the bra pulled away, his hot gaze roved over her full breasts. They were perfect. Two full creamy ice cream cones, with strawberry peaked nipples. And she was blushing right down to them. He was speechless, reaching out to touch them. She shuddered, but it was a good shudder—excited and turned on.

He bent to taste one sweet nipple, drawing it into his mouth. She moaned, shivering under him. When he pulled away, she whimpered.

"Do it again. Please, Billy."

He chuckled against her breast. He hadn't been called Billy since he was twelve, but he was happy to comply. He suckled her while fanning the other nipple with his fingers. She cried out, arching against him.

He reached down to cup her plump mound through her panties. It was hot and damp under his palm. He pressed, and she shuddered, moaning, and he damned near came. She was making him hard as stone.

"Oh, baby," he said, butting against her with his cock, his fingers tracing the cleft of her pussy through her cotton panties. She shivered, her nails digging into his arm.

"Oh, my," she gasped, arching toward his touch.

He groaned, rubbing against her, as he brushed her clit through the material. She whimpered, her legs thrashing. He started to peel off her panties, and she seemed to freeze up again for a moment. Once they were down, she was pressing against him again. His concern that something was off receded as his dick made contact with her thigh.

Bending to kiss her, he was lost. April's lush mouth opened under his as he stroked the plump split peach of her hot pussy. She whimpered, her legs opening as he fingered her labia, his thumb circling her clit. It was stiff, and she was wet and slick. She whimpered into his mouth when he pushed a finger into her.

God, she was tight and pulsing. She clamped down on him, and he groaned knowing how good it would be with her. Settling between her thighs, his cock bumped against her thigh as he bent to kiss her. Despite how much he wanted this to last, he couldn't take much more. He reached in the nightstand for a condom, and sheathed himself while kissing her.

Breaking the kiss, he gazed down at her.

She blushed and looked away, not meeting his gaze when he looked at her.

It bothered him. He wasn't some anonymous dick to pleasure her. Why wouldn't she look at him?

As he started to enter her creamy hot pussy, he saw her tense, felt her tighten around him as if bracing herself for attack, and it became crystal clear to him.

She wasn't teasing him. She was a virgin.

Calling himself a fool, he groaned, holding himself in check. He ached to push past the barrier of her cherry and find completion inside her semi-willing body. She wanted it, but she was afraid. How in the hell had she managed to make it to twenty-eight untouched? She was so damned sexy.

I waited, eyes closed, holding my breath while Will lay atop me. My pulse raced, my nipples were hard sensitive peaks, still wet from his sucking. The juncture of my thoighs was even wetter while it quivered around his head. I needed him deep inside me now.

His cock twitched, throbbing at my body's gate. Why wasn't he deflowering me?

I peeked up at him. He was sweating, and veins stood out on his neck. Something was drastically wrong.

"Well?" I arched against his throbbing cock, gasping when it inched deeper, causing pain.

He groaned. "When were you going to tell me you were a virgin?"

I gazed up at him, stricken. How had he guessed? "I won't be when you get through."

He closed his eyes on a strangled groan. He lowered his head. "You're killing me, precious."

What did he mean by that? I'd hardly even touched him. I tried to gaze at his expression, but it was difficult with his head down that way. Did it mean he wasn't going to? Didn't he fancy virgins? I might not be the most experienced bed partner, but darn it all, he owed me something. I'd hauled my cookies out here for him. He was still hard, throbbing inside my opening, making my pelvic area ultra sensitive. Nerve endings I never knew I had were coming alive, clamoring for him.

Still, he didn't move. I felt like crying from the disappointment, but didn't want to give him the satisfaction. And then, finally he lifted his head. He smiled just a little, in a strained way. Nevertheless, it was a smile. I breathed a sigh of relief, and arched again, wincing when he slipped a bit farther inside me.

He groaned. "Sweetheart, that wasn't fair."

"Not fair?"

"Virgins have to be taken delicately."

I frowned. "Is that your polite way of turning me down?"

He cleared his throat. "No, not at all. You can feel how much I want you, can't you?"

I felt him move, pulling out a bit, just the tip of his hot cock inside me. It felt good, magical. "Yes."

"Good. What I propose is a series of love lessons to get you ready."

My face flamed at the thought, my body tingling. He was suggesting more than a one-time occurrence. Did I want that? My body ached for him now.

"Please." I begged. "I need..."

"Shh," he said, rubbing against me again. "I'll give you all you need, I promise." He kissed me, silencing my protests as his hand moved down to my curls, his fingers finding my clit.

Quivering, I gasped in delight, as he rubbed it harder.

"What about you?" I felt the tip of him throbbing inside me, knowing he had to be far from satisfied. If anything, it was bigger, harder.

"Love lesson number one. There's more than one way to get satisfaction." He tickled my clit. "You have the most incredible pussy, precious," he said, his fingers teasing me. "Say it."

"Pussy?" I asked, embarrassed. I'd never used that word. At least, not out loud.

He chuckled. "And what's inside you, so hard it's about to burst?"

I knew what he wanted me to say, and blushed despite the situation we were in. "Your cock." It felt so naughty saying the word, but sexy, too.

"That's right," he husked, tweaking my clit while another finger circled the rim of my pussy.

Gasping, I quivered around the tip of his cock, my body exploding, my pulsations tugging him deeper. I felt him jerk inside me a bit, making me come once more.

He groaned, rolling us both to the side without pulling out.

My hands went down to his cock, the tip still inside me. Two could play this game. I was gratified to hear him groan as I pumped his shaft.

When he came in his condom, my body pulsed against him. When I came back to earth, he pulled out of me. I peeked at him as he made his way to the bathroom.

The shower turned on, and then he was back for me, startling me as he scooped me off the bed to carry me to the bathroom.

"I can walk, Will."

"Humor me, precious."

He carried me into the shower, setting me on my feet, my breasts erotically rubbing down his hard body. I forgot to breathe for a minute. He bent to kiss me while the hot water rained on us. I felt like laughing and crying at the same time. It was so incredibly erotic.

His rough hands cupped my breasts, his fingers finessing my nipples. They budded, thrusting out for him. When he bent to suck my nipple, it caused a pull deep inside me. I gasped, letting out a moan as he suckled me. His hands found my pussy. Teasing it, he stroked my labia, my clit, and gently thrust a finger into my tight pussy. Then, his little finger teased my anus.

I moaned at the unexpectedly erotic sensation and writhed against his probing fingers.

His cock grew hard against me, pulsing with life. I rubbed against it, starved for him. I quivered as it brushed my pussy and clit. I needed to have it.

Instead, he let me go and reached for a loofah and soap.

Embarrassed, trembling on the brink of coming, I let him wash me. He soaped first one arm, and then the other. When he moved on to my breasts, I whimpered as he scrubbed my hard nipples. They tingled, jutting out harder. He smiled, moving on to my belly, then slicked down to my pussy. The instant the sponge hit my curls I started to come. He pulled the sponge away and I let out a cry of protest.

"Turn around."

I shivered hearing his ragged voice. He was turned on as much as I was, maybe even out of control. He soaped my back, then moved down to my bottom, soaping it, spreading its cheeks, working his way between my legs and finally rubbing my pussy.

Dropping the sponge, he stepped close behind me, his cock touching my bottom, thrusting between my thighs.

"Please."

"I will," he promised.

Ripples took me over as I came, and I gripped his cock with my thighs, watching his cum spurt on the shower wall.

Oh my, to have that happen inside me.

True to his word, he'd taken me every way but inside. I glowed, wondering what the next love lesson would be.

CHAPTER 3

I woke up slowly, feeling warm, languid, and satisfied. A big hand cupped my left breast. My nipple budded, tingled, against his warm palm. An ardent male body spooned against me, his semi-hard manhood nestled between the cheeks of my bottom. Even that contact was arousing.

Will! It hadn't been an erotic dream. It was real. He was real.

My breath caught as he grew bigger against my bottom. He'd pleasured me three times in the night, but still hadn't taken me. Would he make love to me now? As much as it went against my one night stand pledge, I would welcome it. I pushed back against him, his cock riding between my cheeks. His hand cupping my breast squeezed lightly.

Was he awake? Why wasn't he saying something? Or was he waiting for me to make the first move? It didn't seem like his style. He was aggressive, confident, and experienced.

This was awkward. What should I do? I gently disengaged from his hand, hearing him murmur an unintelligible protest. Turning over, I came face-to-face with my naked lover from the night before, except his eyes were closed. He was still sound asleep. He let out a little snore and I grinned. When would I ever get a better opportunity?

I could ogle him all I wanted. I'd only given him sneak peeks last night. His face in slumber was softer. His chest well-muscled and sprinkled lightly with hair. I reached out, lightly touching his warm resilient skin to see if it was as soft as it looked. The covers were already down low around his hips, just not quite low enough. My finger slicked over his washboard flat abdomen to swirl around his navel.

Giving in to temptation, I inched the covers lower to peek at the part of him that lay below. His cock was fascinating, a steel column covered with tanned silky skin. It was stirring, getting bigger as I watched with rapt attention. I reached out to lightly touch the hot velvety head of him, testing it gently with my fingertips. It jerked, swelling even more. Intrigued, I wrapped my hand around the shaft, feeling it pulse with life.

A groan from his lips made me look up. Will was awake, and watching me with a tight smile on his face. I burned with embarrassment.

He reached out to tenderly cup my cheek. "Like what you see?"

Relief rolled through me that he was taking my morning exploration with good grace. Encouraged, I smiled. "You did promise me more love lessons."

"Good grief. I've created a monster," he joked, bending to kiss me.

"Damned straight," I said, surprising myself.

I sighed with pleasure as his mouth claimed mine, and my hand slipped off his cock. He lay back, pulling me on top of him. I sprawled across him, both embarrassed and turned on. He was strong, warm, and solid under me as we kissed. Shamelessly, I thrust my tongue in his mouth, my excitement building as I leaned into him. His hands slipped around my front to shape my breasts. He rolled my nipples between his fingers, making them jut out harder. I stopped kissing him and whimpered as pleasure focused on those tender points.

He put his hands on my waist and effortlessly slid me higher so he could suck on my nipples. My breasts dangled like ripe fruit for his voracious feasting. As his hot mouth closed over my right nipple, a shiver of delight went through me. The tug on my hard nipple caused a pull deep inside like it had last night. My legs spread, my pussy rubbing against his belly, causing a delightful friction. Doubly turned on, I was putty in his hands as he moved to suck my other nipple. My head fell back, and I arched my spine.

When his hot mouth released my nipple, I let out a murmur of protest. But he was lifting me higher so that I was sitting over his face. Embarrassed, I knew he had a close up view of my pussy. Why?

When his tongue flicked out to touch me, my eyes closed, and I moaned. He licked my labia, and then lapped roughly against my clit. I gasped, riding that teasing tongue. His hands were firm on my hips, steadying me, as he started to suck on my labia, drawing first one lip, and then the other into the heat of his mouth. He sucked on my clit, dragging it into his hungry mouth. Then, his tongue slipped into my pussy. My body went spasmodic as I came, my pussy rippling on his tongue as he drew my pleasure out. My eyes rolled back in my head.

When he eased me down to lie beside him, I was limp. He kissed me, and I tasted my essence on him.

Oral sex? Wow! It was the most forbidden, erotic experience I'd ever had. I'd walked in on Edmund and Tiffany doing something similar. Only, Edmund was standing with his pants down around his ankles. Tiffany had been on her knees before him, her mouth on his small cock. At the time, I'd been appalled, vowing I'd never behave in such a scandalous manner. Now, in the afterglow, I was suddenly bit by the notion of trying the same thing on Will—a much more worthy candidate for my attention.

I reached down to touch his erection. It was huge, and full to bursting. My hand closed firmly around the veined shaft as I bent to taste him.

He groaned. "April, you don't have to…"

I ignored his protest as my tongue swirled around the red velvet head of his cock, learning his taste. He was salty and sweet at the same time. The taste was all male. I'd been missing out on passion all these years. I lapped a drop of moisture off the slit, and he groaned again. Emboldened, I started to take him into my mouth.

The sudden clanging of a doorbell made me freeze, the tip of him between my lips.

Will groaned, pulling out. "Damn. That's Matt."

"Your kid brother?" I sat up, my cheeks flaming as the ringing turned into door pounding.

"Afraid so." He slipped out of bed and put on briefs, wincing as he gingerly tucked his full erection into them. Then he slipped on his jeans and grabbed a flannel shirt. He looked at me, his gaze lingering on my bare breasts. "Stay put, I'll get rid of him and come back for more."

I blushed, noting the heat of his gaze. I must look like a total wanton. How embarrassing I'd practically attacked the man, needing so badly to taste him. What did he think of me? I pulled the covers up to my neck. as his gaze lingered on my breasts. Feeling self-conscious, I looked away, but not before noting his frown.

I'd angered him, but that couldn't be helped. This had morphed way out of what I'd originally planned. Suddenly, the idea of a continued alliance sounded dangerous. Maybe it was too tricky for someone of my limited experience to handle. To top it off, I was still technically a virgin.

The moment he left the room, I hopped out of bed and quickly put on my clothes. It wasn't too late to get out of this unscathed. I definitely needed time to consider my options. Luckily, I hadn't given him my real name, so I'd have all the time and space I needed to decide.

I couldn't stop myself from glancing at the rumpled bed with mingled fondness and chagrin. Looking away, I brushed back my hair and gazed at my image in the mirror. My eyes were sparkling, my lips swollen from his kisses, and I was glowing. In short, I looked like a heathen who'd just been tumbled, which was mostly true.

Blushing, I grabbed my shoes and bag, and fled the bedroom. Rushing down the stairs barefoot, I hoped to elude Will's notice. The aroma of coffee being brewed and the sound of genial male voices from the kitchen told me they were in the back part of the house.

Good. If I could slip by the kitchen unnoticed, I'd be home free. Will didn't know my real name. I'd once again be the mistress of my own fate.

Tiptoeing through the living room, I dared a quick look through the open doorway to the kitchen. Will was there, leaning casually against the counter. His pants were zipped I noticed, but his shirt was unbuttoned and his feet were bare. He looked like the confident, satisfied male he was. Sure, he'd come twice, but I had a feeling he hadn't been completely satisfied. In contrast, I'd just discovered my capacity for multiple orgasms, thanks to his sexy love lessons. Were all men such generous lovers? Something told me no.

Will suddenly looked directly at me. Our gazes locked. I froze, busted.

He frowned, pushing away from the kitchen counter as he strode toward me.

Matt turned to look. He was a few years younger, blond where Will was dark, but just as tough. Not a kid anymore.

Will grabbed my hand and tugged me forward. "Come have some breakfast, precious."

I padded into the kitchen with him, embarrassed but determined to brazen it out. "Hello," I said to Matt. Did he know we'd slept together? Of course he did, the twinkle in his brown eyes told me so. I was in a bridesmaid dress, barefoot, and blushing. Will with his bare chest, feet, and heartbreaker smile looked like an advertisement for hot sex. It was pretty damned obvious.

Matt nodded. "Hello, April. Long time no see."

I gasped as he said my name, and my shoes slipped out of my suddenly lifeless fingers.

Matt knew me. I was so shocked, I just stood there, my mouth open. My panicked gaze darted to Will. How would he react to the unmasking? To being fooled? He was calm, smiling even, the twinkle in his blue eyes told me that he already knew. As I stood there coming to grips with the notion, it hit me like a brick wall—he'd known all along. And here I'd thought I'd been so clever. Will had played along with my feeble deception last night, letting me make an absolute fool of myself. Why? For fun, for a joke, to sleep with the nerd girl?

The determined look in his eyes told me he read my anger correctly, and he didn't like it one little bit. His bruised ego was the least of my worries right now. I had to try to get out of this unscathed.

Shoulders stiff with apparent tension, Will bent to pick up my shoes. I broke out of my state of shock, and snatched the silver evening sandals out of his hands. I didn't want to examine my own part in my downfall. Right now, I was too angry for rational thought.

"Now, April," Will started to say.

"I don't want to hear it, Billy." His soft tone made me furious, reminding me our intimacies were based on lies. How could we possibly build anything more on that? Besides, I'd wanted a single night of sex, and that's what I'd gotten. Almost.

"Billy?" Matt asked with a grin.

"Keep out of it," Will warned him, then turned his attention back to me. He reached to touch my cheek.

Matt grinned wider.

I stood, unsure, as Will tenderly cupped my cheek. It was almost enough to make me surrender, but I didn't trust my reactions anymore. And he'd done nothing to gain my trust. *Nothing but pleasure me at his own expense*, a little voice in my head said, but I ignored it. I couldn't deal with this now.

I stepped back as Will frowned, and then I turned to leave. I had to get out of here—now!

Hearing his footsteps behind me, I sped up. Just as I reached the front door, Will caught up to me. He grabbed my hand, bringing me to a halt. I knew his touch, it was imprinted on me. He wasn't hurting me, but he wasn't letting me go, either.

My anger boiled over. "Let me go!"

"No. We need to talk."

"I don't have time to talk now. I have to go." I wracked my mind for an excuse he'd buy. "I'm late for an appointment."

"Okay, later. Meet me at Red's tonight."

His tone was grim, determined. I had no intention of going to Red's, but I wasn't going to tell him that. I needed breathing space, not more pressure.

Luckily, I had an edge on him. He might know my name, but he didn't know where I lived. I wasn't even in the phone book. If I kept my cool and laid low, I'd have all the time I needed to think things out.

"Fine." I tore open the door and stumbled onto the porch, waking the dog, who barked at me.

Will grabbed me, catching me when I might have fallen. "Sit down and put your shoes on, April."

"No time," I protested, tugging away from his grasp. It riled me that he was ordering me around like a child. I turned toward his glower, and let out a startled shriek when his big hands spanned my waist and he picked me up. "Stop that."

He ignored me, sat me on the wide porch railing, and slipped my shoes on my feet, fastening first one sandal, and then the next. I perched there, feeling both touched and bothered. He was taking care of me again, and I wasn't sure I wanted him to.

Then, he lifted me off the railing, stood me before him, and bent to kiss me. I stood still for a moment, my lips stiff beneath his, and then they softened. This I knew, loved, and wanted. His arms came around me, pulling me close. My mouth opened for his probing tongue, reminding me of all the intimacies we'd shared. He growled deep in his throat, and I felt his bulge get bigger. Despite the fact that I didn't quite trust him, and Matt was inside, I went all fluid, sagging against him.

Will broke the kiss, and pushed me away, making me blush.

"Tonight," he said.

I nodded and ran to my car. Getting in, I looked at Will on the porch, handsome as sin and twice as tempting. He was going to be disappointed when I didn't show at Red's tonight, but for my own peace of mind, I had to break away.

CHAPTER 4

Will watched April's silver Audi speed away, and scowled. He could tell when a woman was running away from him, and he didn't like it one bit. Thanks to his brother's big mouth, he'd blown what had promised to be a memorable morning. Of course, Will shouldered part of the blame. He probably should have told her he knew who she was straight off. But last night had been so tenuous, he hadn't wanted to spoil it.

And, finding her a virgin last night had thrown him for a loop. He could have taken what she'd offered, a one-night stand, but damn it, he wanted more. Now he was going to have to work overtime to mend the rift, but mend it he would. One taste of April wasn't enough—not by a long shot.

He headed back into the house to face the ribbing he was probably in for. Matt was pouring himself a refill when Will stomped barefooted back into the kitchen.

His brother flashed him a knowing grin. "Did your girlfriend get off okay?"

Will's spine stiffened at the crude question, but he tried to ignore the double entendre. "Get stuffed." He poured himself a refill, knowing he'd need the caffeine buzz to get through the workday. He hadn't gotten much sleep last night, choosing instead to concentrate on pleasuring April. He'd intended to call Matt in the early morning and postpone the Johnson Hills job. Instead, he'd fallen asleep, only to be awakened by April's warm hand on his cock.

Just the memory of her sweet lips closing over his dick was enough to jump-start him into a hard-on again. Gritting his teeth, he turned his back to Matt and yanked the cream from the refrigerator for something to do.

Matt grabbed the creamer from his hand and poured a liberal amount into his mug. "How come April was so surprised I knew her name? Was she going undercover or something?"

Will snatched the cream back. "It's none of your business, bro."

Matt chuckled. "Oh, I think I hit a nerve. What goes on here, big brother?"

"Simple. Two old acquaintances, getting to know each other again." Will put the cream back in the refrigerator, ignoring his brother's troubled glance. Matt's concern was probably due to Will's acrimonious divorce two years back. He hadn't had a serious relationship since then. But he wasn't about to discuss his sex life with his younger brother.

"Nice. Little April Brooks, who would have thought it? Well, not so little anymore. She has great legs, all the way up to her a—"

"First, you've got no business noticing her legs or any other part of her anatomy. Second, she's not my girlfriend. You know I don't do permanent relationships anymore."

Matt's teasing grin quickly turned into a frown. "You gonna let Tammy spoil you for other women? There are lots of good women out there. It's about time you settled down and gave the folks some grandkids."

Will raised his brow at that little gem. Talk about the pot calling the kettle black. Matt's little black book had to be two inches thick and growing. "I don't see you rushing down the wedding aisle."

"That's different. I'm still looking for Miss Right. I'm playing the field. You've just been moping around for two years since Tammy walked out on you."

Thumping his coffee cup down on the counter, Will knew that Matt's statement was too damned close for comfort. "Come on, let's go to work."

I finished planting the Rosebud's front flower bed and stood back to admire her handiwork. Colorful pansies and petunias winked at me in the late afternoon sunlight. By rights, they should have gone in a month ago, but Aunt Sadie hadn't been in any shape to do it.

Planting the flowers had been almost enough to distract me from thoughts of Will. Almost. Sweet thoughts of him lingered in the back of my mind. My body still glowed, my nipples tingling as I conjured memories of his touch. I'd driven myself mercilessly today trying to exorcise the erotic memory.

This was no way to think things over clearly. I walked back into the old Victorian-style inn to wash up and scrounge something up for supper. Walking through the parlor and dining room made me feel better. They were completely restored, their woodwork crisp, the hardwood floors warm and homey. Sadie's contractors were doing a superb job, even if they were slow to get in touch with me. In fact, they'd yet to make an appearance on my watch. Sadie's murmur about prior commitments was ridiculous in my book. In my world, contracts meant something, and deadlines were met. But not wanting to stress Sadie or cause waves, I'd bitten my tongue.

I walked into the kitchen. Now, this room desperately needed refurbishing. The drains didn't work right and I was in sore need of cupboard and counter space. Still, its cheerful cherry sprigged wallpaper made me smile, reminding me of Sadie. Hopefully, when the refurbishment was done, I would put my stamp on the place, too.

I opened up the refrigerator, noticing there were slim pickings. I'd have to make a run to the store soon.

Later, sitting at the table munching on a cold supper of cheese, crackers, and iced tea, my mind turned to Will once more. Glancing at the clock, I noted it was close to eight. Was he at Red's waiting for me? Did last night mean anything to him? I was dying to know, but I was trying to be strong.

Standing, I marched into the kitchen to do the dishes. That done, I decided to take a drive into town for supplies. Cleaning products for the thorough maintenance I planned to give the old barn, and some groceries to keep me going. As the store was on the way to Red's, it wouldn't hurt to peek and see if Will had actually shown up.

Grabbing my keys off the hall tree, I caught a quick glimpse of myself in the mirror. I was still glowing, darn it. Brushing back a tendril of red hair off my flushed face, I told herself to cool it. My jeans and T-shirt were fine for a run to the store, or Red's, for that matter, not that I was contemplating going inside.

Before I could change my mind, I ran to my car and drove off into the night. Slowing as I neared Red's, I saw that the parking lot was full. Was Will's truck there in among the throng of vehicles? Biting my lip, I thought I saw it among the others.

Drat! I'd have to pull in to be sure.

Slipping into the parking lot, I slowly drove up and down, scanning the dimly lit lot for Will's old truck. Red's was jumping. I rolled down my window and listened to the music drifting on the balmy night air.

And then, I spotted an old pickup parked at the far end of the lot. I inched toward it, and stopped. It was Will's. He was here. For me. I threw the car into park, and craned my neck to look at the bar. My pulse sped up, seeming to echo—*go and get him, go and get him.*

I closed my eyes, dropping my head. This was hard. A part of me wanted to—a big part—but I was scared I would get in over my head.

Someone rapped twice on my car door.

Shrieking, I jumped, and spun around. Not a rowdy drunk, I couldn't handle that right now.

Will was hunkered down at eye level by my window looking so tempting, my breath caught in my throat and my panties got damp. My heart skipped a beat as I gazed at him.

"What are you waiting for, precious, an engraved invitation?" he asked with a soft smile.

I nibbled her lower lip. "No! That is, I'm not sure..."

"Okay." Lines by his eyes crinkled as he focused hard on me. "Please come and ravish me."

Gulping, a heat wave shot through me. I felt ravished by the intensity of his gaze. "I didn't mean..."

"Fine, then how about a dance?"

"I don't want to go inside," I confessed. Seeing the flash of disappointment in his eyes, my willpower began to crumble.

"We've got a starlit dance floor out here." He opened my car door.

How could I refuse an invitation like that? I let him escort me from the car. When he put his arm around me, waltzing me across the parking lot, my doubts melted away. I leaned into his strength, loving the feel of his tender arms around me. My nipples beaded as they brushed against his muscular chest, jutting out at him, tingling. My middle seemed to go fluid, and I felt giddy with desire. How did he work this magic on me? Gasping, I felt the electric touch of his growing erection at the junction of my thighs, my pussy. More stimulation, I burned where we touched.

"Feel what you do to me, precious."

I'd been thinking the same thing about him. My panties got damper as we bumped again, then ground together, little sparks of pleasure rocking through me.

"Oh, Will." I gasped.

The door opened to Red's, barroom noise and a laughing couple came spilling out, intruding on the moment. I froze, suddenly feeling exposed, even though we were only dancing. I stiffened against Will, my arousal teetering on the edge, and by sheer force of will, I pulled myself back from the brink.

He stilled, his arms tightening against me. No doubt, he could feel me pulling away from him, but I couldn't help it. Maybe this wasn't so smart.

When he started to waltz me toward his truck, I blinked up at him. "Where are we going?"

"Away from prying eyes."

Relief rushed through me. "Thank you."

When we reached the shadows by his truck, I immediately felt better. Will's tender embrace felt right, his big hand stroking slowly down my back soothed me. When he bent to kiss me, I lifted up on tiptoes and kissed him back. I licked his lips, sucking on the lower one, hearing him groan. Then his tongue thrust into my mouth, and I sucked on it. His hands cupped my bottom, and he lifted me, holding me tight, rubbing me on his stiff bulge.

Whimpering into his mouth, I ground against him. It was a replay of last night, and my body instantly responded. I pressed tighter, little ripples starting between my legs, waves of pleasure flowing through my pussy. He pressed me tighter, holding me against him. With a gasp, I exploded, his kiss swallowing my cry of pleasure.

Sated, I slumped against him, limp. He was still rock hard against me, his body tense against mine. I peeked up at him. He was sweating.

I'd done it again.

Ravish him, indeed. He flashed me a tight smile.

"My place or yours?" he asked tightly.

"Yours," I found myself blurting.

Another night with him was what I craved. And this time, we'd really do it. I could have all the time I needed to think it over later because he didn't know where I lived.

"Thank God," he grumbled, squeezing me tight. "Get in." Reaching back, he jerked open his truck door.

Shaking my head, I earned a frown from him. "No, I'll take my car."

I'd need a getaway in the morning. It seemed like he was going to object for a moment, then I found myself being speed-walked back to my car. Flashing an embarrassed glance around the parking lot, I caught the other couple in the backseat of a steamed up car.

Shocked, I looked away. Good grief, lust really was in the air.

When we reached my car, Will tugged open the door and all but tucked me inside. I let him move me, feeling utterly bemused. When he fastened my seatbelt, I couldn't stop smiling. I hadn't been this cosseted since I was a child.

The moment he caught my smile, he frowned, straightening. He was probably disgruntled at me being amused by his fussing over me.

"I'll lead the way. Drive carefully, you hear?"

"Yes, sir," I said, smiling wider, amused.

Watching him stalk back to his truck, I wondered if he was going to make love to me or spank me. The tense set of his body and his ground-eating stride sent mixed messages. I let out a helpless laugh. I'd probably let him do either—if it was a sexy paddling.

I waited for Will to drive past, his gaze lingering warmly on me for a moment, and then fell into line behind him. He was going fast again, probably just as excited as I was. When he slowed, so did I. It was important to get there in one piece. We pulled into the driveway, and this time, I wasn't surprised by the hound dog on the porch.

I turned off my car, back to the scene of my first semi-seduction. This time, I wanted it all. Will was standing there, waiting for me when I got out of my car. Without preliminaries, he pulled me into his arms, his mouth claiming mine in a burning kiss.

My arms went around his neck, and I burned against him. A fever seemed to take me over as I pressed closer, my knees going weak. And then, I was floating as he scooped me up into his strong arms, and carried me toward the house.

Ablaze, I pressed kisses against his neck, his chin, feeling his body go hard against mine. He was just as turned on. I was really going to get it. A little zing of excitement and fear went through me, but one thought troubled me. Would he refuse me again, stopping short of making love? I couldn't take it if he did. How far could you push a man before he ravished you? I was about to find out. I sucked on his neck, his breathing growing ragged.

He stomped up onto the porch carrying me, balancing me one-armed, while he opened the door. He started for the stairs, and I reached down to cup the bulge at his crotch. Groaning, he turned, and made for the sofa instead.

Sitting down, he pulled me astride him, facing him. "Is this what you want, minx?"

"Not quite," I said shivering against him. "I want you in me *now*." I leaned forward sucking on his neck again.

He groaned, holding my hips tight, while rubbing against me. "Why are you so impatient, brat?"

"You ought to know. You're the one making me hot." I reached for his shirt. "You're wearing too many clothes, Will."

He shrugged out of his T-shirt and reached for the hem of mine. "Ditto, precious." He tugged my shirt off and tossed it on the floor.

I shivered as our pelvises rocked together, setting off sparks inside me. "Oh my!"

When he gazed longingly at my breasts, hidden behind my bra, I decided to buy all new lingerie. If he thought this plain white cotton was hot, wait until I came to him in black lace.

His big hands cupped my breasts. "Mine."

I let out a pleasured sigh. "Yes."

Then, he reached behind me to unfasten my bra, and I lost all train of thought. He just stared at my bare breasts for a long moment, and I shivered, my nipples beading. They jutted as if he was touching them, and then, he did. Will's warm, work-roughened fingers shaped and pinched my sensitive nipples, tugging on them, lengthening them. My head fell back and I moaned, thrusting them at him.

His mouth closed over one strawberry point, drawing it hard into his hot mouth, and I was gone. He suckled first one and then the other, until little mewling noises poured from my mouth, and I was grinding my pussy, still encased in jeans, against him.

I needed him now!

And then, he stood me up. My knees wobbled, legs bent. He put his shoulder against my middle to prop me up, tugging my jeans and panties down in one swoop. Then, he flung a blanket on the carpet and laid me on it, tugging off my shoes and pants. I let him finish undressing me, pussy contracting, getting wetter. It was throbbing, aching, and I couldn't take my gaze off him.

I watched him shuck his jeans, fascinated. When his cock sprang free of his briefs, my mouth went dry. It was already hard, huge, and all mine.

He came to me then, lying next to me, half on top. He flattened me against the floor. Cupping my breasts, he squeezed them together, licking my stiff nipples, teasing them until I was lifting my hips off the blanket, totally out of my head. His hand slipped down between my legs, his fingers toying with my labia, circling it, and then rubbing my clit before slipping into the wet heat of my pussy.

I gasped, unable to hold still, shaking with excitement as he played with me. "Please," I begged.

He nibbled my neck, his erection rubbing my thigh. "I can't wait anymore, precious. Are you sure?"

"Yes," I said with a whimper as he settled between my legs.

I wanted this more than anything.

He bent to kiss me as the tip pushed into me, and I gasped. In one slow lunge, he thrust inside.

I saw stars, contracting around him. He was so big—maybe too big—uncomfortably big, stretching me tight. But as he lay there, buried deep inside me, his mouth swallowing my moans, ripples of pleasure fluttered through me, easing the discomfort. His tongue surged into my mouth as he started to piston in and out of me. I felt like I was on fire where we were joined, stimulated like never before through the achiness. I gasped at the sweet sensation and snapped my hips up to meet his fevered thrusts.

Driving into me, he growled. "Wrap your legs around me, precious."

I did, clinging to him as my long legs wrapped around his waist. His big hands cupped my bottom, lifting me so he could slam into me harder. I gasped when the position made me take more of him. Throbs of pleasure shot through me as he thrust deeper. Rippling spasms rocked me, little explosions going off deep inside.

Clinging to him, I convulsed, my orgasm pulling him deeper, tugging at his cock as I cried out. He thrust against me twice more, and then he jerked, spurting inside me as he came.

"Mine," he growled.

Still shimmering with after tremors, I let out a little cry of surprise when he flipped us both over so I was now sprawled on top of his hard muscular chest.

I lifted my head and smiled at him. "That was—"

"Mind-blowing," he suggested, raking me with a sultry glance.

"I was going to say nice. But now that you mention it, mind-blowing does fit."

"That's not the only thing that fits," he said with a smile.

"I was just thinking the same thing, cowboy," I said, kissing him.

He patted my bottom, making me smile.

"Hold that thought, precious." He slipped me off him to lay on the blanket.

I rose up on one elbow to watch him stride toward the kitchen. "Where are you going?"

"Arranging a little surprise for you."

"Surprise," I said, sitting up. I was sore, but it was wonderful. "What is it?"

He smiled, flicking the remote to light the gas fireplace. "A little atmosphere would be nice, don't you think?"

"Oh, yes," I said, smiling.

I watched him walk naked into the kitchen, wondering what he was up to. I couldn't take my eyes off him. He was magnificent, and all mine.

A few moments later, he came back and reached for my hand. "Come."

I'd already done that, I thought with a sassy grin, but rose, taking his hand. I let him lead me through the house, walking freely naked. When we went through the kitchen and onto the back deck, I gave him a second look.

"I've got a nine foot tall privacy fence, April, and no neighbors. You could come sunning out here at noon and nobody would be the wiser."

That explained his all-over tan, I thought with a giggle. He led me through the patio door and out onto the large deck. Chinese lanterns hung from the rafters, lighting the nook. A swirling hot tub caught my eye. Its wide deck was flanked with lit candles. Jasmine and vanilla, I decided, inhaling the fragrance. A teak table was set with a chilling bottle of bubbly in an ice bucket, two champagne flutes, and a tray of plump chocolate covered strawberries.

I could hardly believe my eyes. Will had gone to so much trouble for me.

He picked a red rose from the bouquet on the table.

I stood transfixed as he brushed the velvety petals softly against my cheek.

"Thank you. I love my surprise," I said with tears in my eyes, touched. He'd wanted my first time to be special. And it had been because of him.

He linked his fingers with mine, squeezing, then led me to the tub. "Come on, let's take a dip."

I climbed in, sighing when the swirling water soothed my tender bottom.

He watched me. "Feel okay?"

"Yes, I feel wonderful." I smiled at him to relieve his fears. I was just a little tender.

"Good." He nodded and walked to the table. He popped the cork on the champagne. He poured the bubbly.

I smiled, thinking this was perfect. Will was perfect.

I took the glass he handed me and took a sip. It was intoxicating, but not as intoxicating as Will.

He slipped into the hot tub beside me, clinking his champagne glass with mine. "To beginnings."

"To beginnings," I agreed, taking another sip. That was just what this was, the beginning of my love life, and Will was the perfect man to lead me down that path.

He put his glass on the table and reached for a plump strawberry, feeding it to me.

My teeth closed on the soft fruit, tasting the juice bursting onto my tongue. I licked my lips, his eyes flaring as he watched me.

He lowered the half-eaten berry, rubbing it against my nipple. Then, he bent to lick off the juice. Lapping at my budding nipple, he drew it into his mouth. I moaned, gripping his shoulders. His hand drifted between my legs, testing my readiness.

I gasped as he tweaked my clit, his fingers smoothing over my vulva, dipping into my pussy. I cried out, rippling against his blunt finger, my hand finding his cock under the swirling water. It was hard, sticking up.

My hand curled around him, and I moaned. "Please now. I need you now."

His hands spanned my waist, and he lifted me up and over him, gently settling me on his shaft.

I let out a moan as my pussy gradually swallowed his cock. He was so big, I felt tight to the point of bursting again. As I lay against him, trembling, my heart racing, I slowly adjusted.

I rocked against him, testing the fit, whimpering at the exquisite pleasure. My swollen clit brushed against him with every move. His big hands gripped my bottom, guiding my movements. I closed my eyes and held on for the ride as he started moving me faster.

My pussy fluttered around his thrusting cock as my orgasm built. I wrapped my arms around him, my fingers kneading his strong shoulders. I heard his groan, his whole body seeming to tighten under mine.

He thrust harder, pressing me tight against him, and I came with a gasp, calling his name.

CHAPTER 5

Will couldn't stop staring. April looked so beautiful, sleeping in the early morning light. She was sprawled half on top of him, and his arm was nearly numb, tingling with pins and needles.

Still, he didn't want to wake her. They hadn't made it up to the bedroom last night. He was insatiable for her, and she wasn't far behind. He'd stuck a tie on the doorknob during the middle of the night, a Do Not Disturb signal for Matt. Nothing would stop Will from teaching April all the love lessons she could handle. He delighted in taking the time to pleasure her properly.

Smoothing a hand down her exquisite body, he cupped her full breast in his palm. Her breasts were perfect and erotic. Everything about her was erotic. His fingertips brushed her nipple and it budded. She was so responsive! He got hard just watching. Her legs flowered open, and she murmured his name in her sleep as she edged closer to him.

Happy to oblige, he reached down to play with her pussy. She was wet and creamy.

Listening to her breath coming in little pants, he leaned forward, fascinated as her eyes fluttered open. The look of desire she focused on him made him harder.

"Morning, precious."

She stretched and smiled, pressing her breast into his hand. "What a nice way to wake up."

"Always willing to accommodate," he said, rolling between her open thighs, and plunging into her.

She gasped in surprise and tightened around him, reminding him how newly opened she was. He instantly gentled his stokes, and she loosened around him.

"Easy does it, babe."

Starting a slow rocking motion, he kissed her, swallowing her moans of pleasure. April's hips snapped up to meet his thrusts as she took him deeper. Her pussy was rippling around him, milking him as she came. He groaned, holding her hips tight as he spilled his load into the condom. It was a good thing he had a large supply, but at the rate they were going, he'd have to replenish it soon.

Breathing hard, he rolled over, taking her with him. Her body cushioned on top of him. He rubbed a gentling hand down her silky smooth back, stopping to cup the generous swell of her sweet ass.

"Which love lesson was that?" she asked with a bemused chuckle.

"I've lost count, precious."

There was a thud outside, followed by a sharp bark.

April stiffened atop him. "What was that? Do you think Buck's okay?"

"It's probably a stray squirrel or the mailman," he hurried to reassure her, but her tension didn't abate.

She slipped off him, reaching for the shirt she'd discarded. "Please go see."

Will stifled a groan of impatience. If it would relax her, it was worth it. She didn't realize it, but Buck caused a ruckus for all kinds of reasons—usually squirrels.

He smiled at her. "If it'll make you happy."

She looked so adorable wearing just a shirt and a blush. She was deliciously tumbled, and he couldn't wait to do her again.

He hurried to the door and looked outside. Matt was perched on the porch railing sipping a Styrofoam cup of takeout coffee while he petted Buck.

"Well, damn," Will said with a grumble.

"What's wrong? Who's out there?" she asked.

Will turned and spotted April with that deer in the headlights look again. And she was already half dressed.

"My pain in the ass brother."

She blushed, standing as she pulled on her jeans. "Oh, my. Is it that late?" Her gaze darted toward the clock. "Eight o'clock! Good gracious, I've got to go."

Will took a step toward her. She was freezing up on him again. No way was he going to take that lying down. "Don't you worry, babe. I'll get rid of him, and we can have our morning delight."

"No!" she protested, grabbing her purse. "I have business in town."

He stood there, frustrated as hell, while she prepared to run. Tearing her clothes off right now and paddling her cute butt until she admitted they had a relationship going was not PC, but that's what he felt like doing. Seemed like she was reducing him to a one-night-stand again, and he didn't like it one little bit. Later, he'd set things straight between them.

When she approached him by the door, he merely raised a brow. "Later," he vowed.

"Right," she murmured, not meeting his gaze.

He jerked open the door so she could leave. As she brushed past him and onto the porch, he reminded himself that even if she didn't realize it, this affair wasn't over. Not by a long shot.

"Morning, April," Matt said, standing as she stepped out on the porch.

April blushed and hurried toward the stairs. "Good morning."

Will turned and scowled at Matt. "Hey, bonehead, can't you read the signs?"

Matt shrugged. "Relax. I didn't knock. Besides, it's business, big bro."

Stopping in her tracks, April turned to ask, "Sign?"

Matt's gaze flashed to the striped necktie wrapped around the doorknob. "Sure. A tie on the door."

She gazed at the tie, her eyes narrowing. She threw an outraged look at Will before hurrying down the stairs.

I sat at the desk in my study, going over the checklist one more time. Compiling it this morning had helped take my mind off my confusing love life.

I was still bothered by Will advertising our assignation with a tie on the door. He probably did it all the time with other women. Damn it all, now that I'd gotten what I wanted, I wasn't happy about being just one more notch on his bedpost.

Sighing, I looked over my list. Sadie's contractors, Ace Builders, were good, but they were too darned slow. Probably balancing too many jobs at once and giving me short hours, I guessed. I will put a stop to that, and bring this job in on time and budget.

When they arrived, I'd be ready with my list of demands.

Hearing the crunch of tires in the drive, I hopped up, list in hand, ready to do battle. Hurrying through the parlor and foyer, I took a deep breath to calm myself. I wore one of my business suits. Taupe with tan pinstripes, I looked every inch the businesswoman. I'd even pulled my hair back in a severe bun. I was ready.

I walked out onto the porch, and my heart skipped a beat as the truck parked in the driveway.

Will? How had he found me? I'd recognize his truck anywhere.

What did he want with me, a roll in the hay, or an argument? I wasn't ready to climb back into bed just yet. But, we hadn't actually made it to bed.

Shaking off that errant thought, I watched him climb out of his truck and stalk toward me, striving for a way to divert him. His walk was brisk and purposeful, his expression determined.

On rubbery knees, I moved closer to the steps to ward him off. "Will, what are you doing here?"

He stepped onto the porch, his smile widening. "Business." He handed me a card.

I looked at it, disbelieving.

Ace Contractors

William Shepard, Head Contractor.

"But, it can't be."

Watching me cautiously, he frowned. "What's the matter, don't you believe I'm a contractor? Trust me, I've got the skills."

"That's not the issue, and you know it, so don't try to change the subject." My nose wrinkled as I frowned at him. "Why didn't you tell me?"

He shrugged. "Would you have in my position?"

"Probably not," I had to answer, hating the deception. "I don't think this is going to work, Will," I said, backing away.

Inching forward, he shook his head. "I've got a contract. Besides, you'll have hell to pay getting another contractor that's half as good."

His confident statement took some of the wind out of my sails. He was good. I'd already decided that, but I wasn't about to admit it. I'd been thinking Sadie's contractor was a pro, but that didn't mean I'd put up with his interminable delays. If he forced my hand, I'd outsource the job or pick up a hammer and do it myself.

"Conceited, aren't you?"

"No." He grinned. "I just know my strengths and weaknesses."

"Such as?" I asked, intrigued.

His intense gaze focused on me, looking deep into my eyes before sweeping over my body. "You've had a sample of my strengths, precious." He winked at me. "My weakness at the moment is a sexy redhead."

Flustered and flattered by his attention, I stepped back another pace. I couldn't help it, my pulse sped up, and my nipples tingled, budding. I was suddenly glad I'd worn the blazer so he couldn't see how he affected me. "Well, if I'm stuck with you, come in. I have something we need to go over."

Turning, I walked back into the inn, making a beeline to my office. I didn't have to look back to see if he followed. I could feel him. His presence was imprinted on my soul.

Entering the open door to the study, I stopped in front of my desk and gestured toward a chair. Will dropped into it, and sat eyeing me cautiously. I could feel his coiled tension, and it made me nervous. Handing him the list, my hand brushed his, and I sucked a deep breath. Sparks shot between us. My nipples tingled again, and my knees grew weaker. Trying to look unfazed, I perched on the edge of my desk.

I held my composure. "As you can see, I've come up with a checklist for this project. I'll expect you to abide by it, if you want to keep this job." I watched him give the list a cursory once over, his brow lifting, probably at one particular entry.

He looked back up at me and smiled. "Done."

His instant capitulation left me speechless for a second. "Just like that?"

"Yes, precious, just like that."

The pet name made me think of rumpled sheets and bare skin.

Driving back the memory, I frowned at him. "Let's keep this all business, please."

"Right," Will said, standing. "I've got some unfinished business for you." He closed the distance between us.

"Now, Will." My eyes widened as I scooted back on the desk. I knew exactly what he wanted. "We have to stick to business."

"Don't worry, precious, I mean business." He bent to kiss me, silencing my sputters.

As his demanding mouth slanted over mine, I went stiff for a moment, and then my resistance crumbled. I wanted this as much as he did.

My arms went around his neck, pulling him closer. I opened my mouth for his tongue, and it surged inside, coaxing my surrender.

He pushed the blazer off my shoulders, and I moaned as his rough hands cupped my breasts through the silk blouse. He unbuttoned it, tugging it and my bra straps down, entrapping my arms with them. I struggled, frustrated because I wanted to touch him, and just a bit shocked. He was so intense, dominant. When his hot mouth captured my nipple, drawing hard on the tender peak, I forgot my concerns. I squirmed against him, the restraints adding to my excitement. I was at his mercy as he sucked and teased my nipples repeatedly until I was a quivering pile of desire.

Pushing up my skirt, he pulled my panties aside, his fingers teasing my pussy. I was wet for him. I wanted him so bad, but he wouldn't take me. Aching for him, I whimpered, trembling as he played with me. Out of my mind with desire, I pressed against his tantalizing fingers.

"You're mine," Will said with a growl, lifting his head from my nipple. "Say it."

"I'm yours," I said with a gasp as he unzipped his pants and entered me in one frantic thrust.

"Yes." I moaned, wrapping my legs around him as he cupped my bottom with his big hands.

Holding me still, he slammed into me. Gasping, rippling, tugging at his surging cock, I exploded, seeing stars behind my closed eyes.

He surged into me once more with a hoarse cry of completion.

CHAPTER 6

Two days later, I sat in the passenger seat of Will's truck as we drove into town together. I needed to pick up my mail and Will needed supplies—hardware and condoms.

It was our public debut as a couple, and I was proud to be sitting by his side, even if I was a bit nervous about people's reactions. I still wasn't used to having an affair, being some possessive man's lover. Of course, I felt pretty possessive about Will, too. Even so, I wasn't completely comfortable with people knowing we were having an affair. Matt knew, of course. And the rest of Will's crew had picked up on the strong vibes between us. They were very nice and respectful, but it made me uneasy.

Will parked on a side street halfway between the post office and Baker's Hardware Store, and turned to smile at me. "How about a bite of lunch after we run errands?"

My stomach grumbled at the mention of lunch. I was famished.

"Okay," I hurried to say, slipping out of the truck.

When he fell into step beside me, I glanced at him. It would take twice as long if he tagged along with me.

"Why don't you go get what you need at the hardware store? I'll check Sadie's post office box and meet you back here."

We came to a halt as passersby walked around us. I thought Will was going to argue for a minute when he frowned at me. Then, he nodded and dropped a brief burning kiss on my lips, uncaring of prying eyes.

As he walked away, I stood there, gathering my wits about me. Turning, I headed to the Post Office with a smile on my face. I really was falling for him, and I wasn't sure the feeling was reciprocated.

I decided to worry about it later as I stepped into the building. I nodded at Mr. Baxter, my eighth grade algebra teacher, and turned toward the row of boxes. Using the little silver key, I opened it to see it burgeoning with junk mail. Aunt Sadie was the con man's dream pigeon. I got sales pitches by the score.

I took the pile to a table nearby to sort. Utility bills went into the keep pile, and junk promptly went into the waste receptacle. As I was nearing the bottom of the heap, I came upon a typed envelope addressed to me. I tore it open, and my knees buckled.

Edmund!

It was a typed, single-spaced love letter with his signature neatly penned on the bottom. I stared at it in disbelief.

April Dearest,

Please come back immediately. Don't do this to me. Our work and the school are suffering. Do our years together mean nothing to you?

As ever,

Edmund

My spine stiffened. How dare he demand I return—to say nothing of trying to guilt me into taking him back? It was more than a little creepy. It brought back fresh waves of shame and anger as my mind flashed back to the humiliating scene I'd walked in on. Tears stung my eyes.

Noticing others were looking at my shocked reaction, I stuffed Edmund's letter in the middle of the utility bills and marched out.

I walked back to Will's truck in a daze.

Will walked through the lumber warehouse behind Baker's Hardware Store, looking through the rack of fine hardwoods. He was seeking the perfect specimen for his gift to April.

He was going to renovate her bedroom personally, right down to custom woodwork and furniture. He'd build their mahogany four-poster bed himself. Looking at a thick mahogany board, the thought stopped him short.

He was already thinking of it as their bed. Strangely enough, the thought of a commitment didn't make him want to run for the hills like it would have a few weeks ago. April had brought about the difference in his attitude toward monogamy. He might not be ready to pop the question, but he was smart enough to know he held a precious jewel in his hands.

After checking the board, he put it down, and filled out his order blank by hand. Baker's hardware did things the old fashioned way, not going for computerized ordering yet. It fit the slower pace of the community.

He turned, walking from the warehouse into the hardware store.

Greg Baker, a big burly former classmate of his, was busy behind the contractor's desk filling an order for Ron from Cotter's Plumbing.

Will stood back, waiting a bit impatiently. He was over eager to get back to April.

Ron looked over his shoulder and smiled. "Well, speak of the devil."

"What's up?" Will asked.

"You having your annual birthday bash at Red's this weekend? We were wondering."

Greg grinned. "*He* was wondering. I don't care either way."

"You've been kind of busy lately."

On his birthday, Will usually asked a few pals to Red's for beer and pool. Funny, he hadn't even realized his birthday was coming up. He decided to ignore Ron's fishing for information about April. This party would be a perfect time to introduce April to his friends.

"The party's on for eight o'clock. Stop on by if you can, and bring your wives. It'll be a couple's party this year."

Greg nodded. "Sounds good. The wife's been complaining I never take her anywhere."

"I'll be there, too," Ron chimed in. "Oh, by the way, have you got a firm work list set for my renovations at The Rosebud?"

Will grinned, thinking of April's checklist and the sweet way they'd come to an understanding. "Sure do. How about if I have Matt run it by your shop later today?"

"Sounds good. See ya." He walked out of the shop.

Will nodded and slid his order slip across the counter. "I've got a special order for you."

Greg took the blank and let out a whistle. "I see that you're going for the expensive stuff."

Hearing Greg's surprised tone, Will made some quick mental calculations on how he could shift men and materials around. He'd free up one of the trucks to go on a ninety mile run to pick up the high-grade lumber if needed.

"Do you think you'll be able to fill it? I want nothing but the best for this client."

"Sure, I'll get it for you, but it might take me a week to get it all in."

Will was relieved he wouldn't have to delay April's job. "No problem. I've got a lot of other rooms to renovate first. Give me a call when it comes in."

He turned to leave the store, whistling. He hadn't felt this good in years, and he knew April was the reason. She'd made life sparkle again.

The bell tinkled as he left the building, and he gave a wave to Earl behind the counter. "See you this Saturday."

He walked down the sidewalk, looking forward to a long lunch with April, and maybe a little romance later on.

"Hey, bonehead," a laughing woman's voice yelled.

His kid sister's teasing voice stopped him in his tracks, and he turned to look behind him.

Courtney was bearing down on him, a bolt of silky red fabric tucked under her arm, flapping in the breeze as she jogged toward him. He looked past her to the frosted window of Spice, the high-class sexy boutique she worked at, and frowned. He wasn't sure he liked his kid sister working there, even if she was a successful lingerie designer.

"Hey, yourself. I see you're hard at work."

"Of course." She wiggled her eyebrows for dramatic effect. "There's never a dull moment at Spice. I'm working on a new line of teddies for the next season. You like?"

"Pretty stuff," he admitted with a reluctant grin, thinking how sexy April would look draped in it. "So, is that why you're chasing me down, to show me your new wears?"

"Don't get sassy with me, big brother." She stuck her tongue out at him. "Mom's been trying to reach you for days to make sure you're coming to your birthday dinner Friday at six." She broke into a sly grin, adding, "Oh, and she told me to tell you to bring a friend."

Another birthday obligation he hadn't even thought of. With his mind on the bedroom, he'd forgotten all about the barbeque his parents liked to throw for his birthday.

"A friend." God, did the whole town know about his new love? He wasn't quite sure he wanted to spring the whole family on April yet. They might just scare her off in their rush to get him hitched.

Courtney smiled wider. "Yes. You know, a certain lady client?"

"And let Mom give her the third degree?" He shook his head. "I'm not quite that stupid."

"Look at it as a bonding experience. We all had to go through it. She asked my fiancé what his intentions were the first time they met. Talk about embarrassing, but we laugh about it now."

"Right," he said doubtfully. "Matt and I are going to have to have a little talk about gossiping."

"Hey, he only told me and Mom. I wormed it out of him after I heard rumors that she picked you up at Red's last weekend."

He frowned at the possible aspersion on April's character, but the open smile on his sister's pretty face told him she'd meant no insult. "For your information, little miss snoop, she didn't pick me up. It was mutual."

Her brown eyes widened. "Oh, I didn't mean to imply anything wrong. I think it's great that you found someone special. I couldn't be happier." She reached up on her tiptoes to kiss his cheek and gave him a hug.

He hugged her back. A gasp behind him captured his attention. There was something familiar about it. Light, breathy.

April.

He pulled away from Courtney's hug, and turned to find April climbing in the backseat of a taxicab. She gave him a tearful glance. A mingling of fury and pain flashed on her pretty face before she turned her back on him.

He felt as if he was trapped in quicksand, like he couldn't move, as Courtney let out a little sound of dismay beside him.

April was gone. Obviously because she'd thought Courtney was someone other than his sister. How could she have jumped to such an asinine conclusion?

"Oh no, was that..." Courtney bit her lip.

He let out a heavy breath, as the weight of the world seemed to pile on his shoulders. "I'm afraid so. That was April."

"Then, she thinks..."

"I've never given her any reason to doubt me." His gut tightened as he recalled her turning away from him. "She could have at least given me the benefit of the doubt."

"Now, Will." Courtney placed a soft hand on his arm. "Don't take this rejection to heart. You owe it to her to find out the truth. Who knows? She may have been burned by love before."

"Love," he scowled, trying to downplay his emotions. "Who said anything about love? We're talking about a little thing called trust here. Obviously, she doesn't trust me."

"Do you want me to talk to her?"

He shook his head. "No. I'll deal with this. I'll see you at the folks' at six on Friday."

"Good luck," she called after him.

He strode to his truck. It was time to clear the air. He wouldn't have another relationship built on lies and distrust.

Half an hour later, I was sitting on a sofa in The Rosebud's parlor, sipping a cup of green tea in an attempt to calm down. The image of Will standing in the arms of another woman wouldn't fade. I'd been wandering towards the hardware store, Edmund's odious letter in hand, when I saw Will in the pretty blonde's embrace. And he seemed damned happy there. The woman's arm was wrapped around him, and she'd lifted up on her tiptoes to kiss his cheek. He laughed at something she'd said, patting her back.

That had been the last straw as far as I was concerned. Men!

In a fog of emotional pain, I'd hailed a cab. On the way back to the Rosebud, I kept watching for Will out the rearview mirror, but didn't see him. Was he still chatting up the blonde bimbo, drowning his sorrows at Red's, or mad enough to spit?

A crunch of tires outside told me he was back. I tensed again. Dang the man. I was through letting men affect me.

Trembling, I put down my teacup, and tried to calm myself. It didn't work. Will's ground-eating stride was loud on my hardwood floors. He was coming, and he was pissed.

A frisson of apprehension shot through me. Even though I was the injured party, I had good reason to be angry with him. Who was that woman? Was Will carrying on with her, too? A million questions whirled around in my head. Questions I should have posed out in the street. It was killing me not knowing.

When he plopped down next to me on the sofa, I inched away, staring into his angry eyes. His big hands spanned my waist, and I let out a startled yelp as he bodily picked me up, and plopped me onto his lap.

Excuses I'd expected. Being manhandled, I hadn't. I wasn't some rag doll he could just move around at will. I turned to tell him just that, but his troubled look stopped me.

He frowned. "What's the matter with you? Don't you have any more faith in my loyalty than this? I want to know what's put this bee in your bonnet. Spill it."

My waist heated where his hands touched me, making me even more flustered. His hard heat under my bottom made me ultra aware of his masculinity. Still, I was in a fighting mood, even though he was making noises like he was the wronged one. Faith, loyalty? Those were words Edmund used to throw around, too. I refused to be duped by a man again.

"Do you have to manhandle me?"

"Yeah, I do." His hands tightened on my waist. "And don't change the subject, April."

"Who was that grabby woman?"

A nerve ticked in Will's tight jaw. "Grabby woman?"

"Yes, *grabby woman*. In the street with her hands all over you."

"And were my hands all over her?" he asked.

"Well, no." I met his confident gaze, my anger starting to fade. He didn't come off as a cheating scoundrel. "But you weren't exactly fighting her off."

"You're jealous?" His eyes crinkled as his mouth kicked up in a reluctant smile.

"I am not." When he didn't answer, I asked, "Well?"

"That grabby woman, as you called her, is my kid sister, Courtney."

My face heated. "That was Courtney?"

"Sure was."

Stifling an embarrassed groan, I said, "Sorry. I haven't seen her in years, and I didn't recognize her. I was upset and jumped to the wrong conclusion."

"What had you so upset?"

I really didn't want to talk about this, but I knew he wouldn't be easily diverted. Squirming, I felt him tighten beneath me, tensing for battle. I might win a few skirmishes, but I wouldn't win the war.

Sighing, I blurted, "I got a letter today from Edmund."

"Edmund?"

His eyes widened in surprise. "Yes, Edmund. My ex-fiancé."

"Your ex-fiancé?"

On edge, I snapped, "If you're going to make me repeat everything, this is going to take a really long time. We were engaged for three years."

He quirked a brow. "During which time, you remained untouched?"

Embarrassed by his continued curious study, I shrugged and looked away. "You said it yourself. The guy I was with was an amateur. I'd thought he wasn't interested in sex. Turns out, he wasn't interested in having it with me. After we broke up, I left my job at the college and came back home to run The Rosebud. The rest, you know."

"What happened?"

"Oldest story in the world. I caught him with another woman."

"Oh, babe."

I blinked back tears of frustration. "You don't have to feel sorry for me."

"I feel a lot of ways for you," he said, his hand rubbing my bottom. "Sorry isn't one of them."

Hearing the sincerity in his voice, I turned to glance at him, and then bent to kiss him. My mouth slanted over his, my tongue sought access to his mouth. My feminine power returned when he let me ravish him. My hands slipped under his shirt, kneading his resilient skin. His muscles flexed below my fingers. My secret was out, and I felt free all of a sudden. I tasted him, my tongue licking at his flat nipples as I opened his fly.

When I captured his burgeoning cock in a confident grasp, his startled groan made me smile. It was hard, pulsing in my hand. I jacked my hands up and down, testing it, teasing it, and then, I sank on my knees. He groaned as my tongue flicked around his red velvety head. My mouth opened, taking the head, feeling him grow hotter and harder. It was so wicked, forbidden, what I was doing, and it excited me.

When he pulled me up, I stepped out of my panties and climbed onto his lap. I sighed as his hard length slipped into my pussy. His hands were firm on my bottom, guiding me as I bounced up and down on his cock. I whimpered as waves of pleasure rippled through me. He kissed me as I exploded, swallowing my cry of pleasure as I came.

I snuggled in his arms in the afterglow. His big hand slid down my back, soothing me. I did trust him, completely, I realized.

"It's my birthday Saturday," he said.

"Happy birthday, baby." I smiled against his warm chest. "I'll have to bake you one of my special chocolate cakes."

"It sounds almost as delicious as you, precious. I have an annual birthday bash at Red's. Nothing fancy, just pool, pizza, and beer. I'm going to try to class it up this year and make it a couple's party. I'd like you to go with me."

So, he thought of us as a couple. It reinforced my feelings of commitment.

"I'd like that a lot."

"Good," he rumbled with a relieved sigh. He stroked my back again, and then stopped. "Oh, there's also a family dinner at my parent's house. Would you want to go with me?"

I smiled at his obvious tension. He was nervous about me meeting his folks. It was endearing.

"I'd love to."

CHAPTER 7

Coming in from cleaning out the barn, I noticed the landline phone ringing. I rushed to answer it just as Will strode into the kitchen to pick it up.

Smiling at him, I snatched the receiver and gasped out a breathless, "Hello."

The pervert on the other end started his heavy breathing again.

Scowling, I muttered, "Jerk," and plopped the receiver back in its cradle, at which point the end cap popped off and rolled across my new granite countertop.

Damn. I lunged forward to catch it, snagging it with my fingertips, and did my best to reattach it to the ancient wall phone. It needed replacing. The whole phone system needed to be redone. Reaching for the scotch tape, I wound a few strands around the mouthpiece.

Why did the perverted kook have to keep calling me? It was the sixth such call in as many days. A thought that it could be Edmund flitted through my mind. He didn't have the guts to approach me in person, I knew already. But would he do something so vindictive?

Anyway, he'd probably moved on to another woman by now, and good riddance. Then, out of the corner of her eye, I caught movement. Startled, I let out a gasp until I realized it was Will. I forgot he'd been standing there. How much had he seen, heard?

I turned to look at him. He was gazing at me with a concerned frown. Probably wondering if he was getting involved with some kind of nut case, I decided.

"What's wrong?" he asked. "Who was that?"

I wrinkled my nose. "Nothing's wrong, Will. It's just some heavy breather trying to scare me."

"And you've had these calls before?" he asked, his eyes narrowing.

"They've been going on for about a week," I said, noting his concerned frown deepening, and hurried to reassure him. "It's nothing, really."

"Any idea who's doing it?" he asked undeterred.

"No." I wished like heck that I knew. "As you can see, I'm not exactly equipped with the latest technology."

"Have you reported it to the police?"

"And tell them what? Some pervert is huffing and puffing at me? For all I know, it could be an asthmatic who's been misdialing." Watching him roll his eyes, I knew my reasoning sounded lame. But, I felt kind of funny about reporting this. The cops would probably think I was overreacting, a hysterical female. After all, the man hadn't actually said anything or threatened me.

"How about changing your number then?" he suggested.

"I can't do that. It might hurt my business. Who knows how many past guests have this number. Besides, I've got a new advertising campaign slated to start in a few weeks with this number."

"Now, listen—"

"Calm down," I cut in. When he fell silent, I hurried to say, "I'm going to get a new phone system with caller ID and an answering machine so I can screen my calls."

"When?" he asked, his determined gaze focused on me.

I looked straight back at him, wanting to make the point that I was in charge of my life. I could handle this little crisis. "I'll get around to it soon."

"Well, see that you do," he said, going back to work.

"Yes, sir," I teased, watching him walk away, tool belt slung low on his hips. He still had the power to make me weak in the knees with just one look.

Half an hour later, Will walked into the office where I was sorting files. "I called a friend at the police station and made a preliminary complaint for you regarding the prank calls."

I looked up, startled. "I never asked you to do that."

"It needed to be done."

My nose wrinkled as I frowned at him. Gazing at the determined set of his jaw, I acknowledged he really did take good care of me. So, I refrained from comment, knowing he'd done it with the best of intentions. It was just like him to take it upon himself to call the police.

"Well, what did he say?" I asked a bit grudgingly.

"He suggested you sign up for caller ID right away, and log any other prank calls. After you make a list, he'll deal with the miscreants. I'm going to make a run to town now. Why don't you come along? We'll sign you up, and get you a new phone."

I gazed at the period piece on my desk. I did need a new, efficient phone system for the inn, one with all the latest bells and whistles.

"Fine." This outing would be a good time to buy the new lingerie I was craving. "Afterwards, I want to do a little shopping. I'll take a taxi home."

"Okay. Let's go." He took my elbow.

Drawn along with him, I grabbed my purse off the desk. "Don't you need to tell Matt where we're going?"

"He knows. Don't worry, he's got things covered here."

So, it was already planned, and my capitulation was taken for granted. I wasn't worried about Ace Builder's timeline. They'd been working ahead of schedule since me and Will had our show down.

I was silent on the ride into town, taking a few sidelong glances at Will. The tense set of his shoulders told me he was taking this phone prankster seriously. To tell the truth, I'd been bothered by it, too. The renovations would be over in a few weeks, and I'd be alone again. The idea of someone playing phone games with me while I was alone at night was creepy. Will's aggressive attitude was warranted, I decided. The sooner they nipped the caller's antics in the bud, the better.

Parking on Wood Avenue in front of the phone company, Will turned to look at me. "You ready to do this?"

"Sure, let's go," I said, drawing strength from his presence.

He nodded and got out.

I joined him on the sidewalk, and we headed into the phone company, hand-in-hand. Walking up to the counter, I noticed Mrs. Hall was still working. Seventy if she was a day, the lady exuded warmth and good cheer. I had taken piano lessons from her in the sixth grade. My face heated as the lady's twinkling eyes focused on my hand in Will's.

"April, honey, I heard you were back in town. How are things at the inn?"

"Fine," I murmured. "I need to purchase a new phone system right away, if it wouldn't be too much trouble."

"And she needs caller ID, one equipped for it today. She's been getting prank calls."

"Oh, dearie dear. There's been a lot of that going on. Don't you fret, I'll get you fixed up right away."

Half an hour later, I stepped outside with Will at my side, thrilled with my fancy new phone system. It was expandable to the guest rooms if I should decide to run lines up there. "Thanks for helping me pick out the phones, and for contacting the police for me, too." I said, meaning every word.

"I'm always here for you, precious, remember that."

"I will."

We turned to walk down Main Street. I noticed a boutique with frosted windows and a sign that said 'Spice.' Gorgeous lingerie hung in the window.

Intrigued, I came to a halt. "What's this shop? I've never seen it before." I was startled to see a stain of red on Will's face.

"It's new. Spice sells lingerie and other things—sex toys and such," he said, chuckling when I blushed. "Monica Landers owns it."

"Modest Monica?" I was shocked and intrigued. Monica had been a whiz at home economics, winning prizes for her clothing designs. Apparently, she had only grown as a seamstress.

Intrigued, I couldn't help trying to peer though the frosted windows to no effect. "Let's go in."

"Why not," he said, his eyes darkening. "I'll buy you some special presents."

"Oh, goody. My very own sex toys."

He took my hand and led me to the door. Opening it, a bell tinkled. I smiled looking at it.

Will stopped, and I almost blundered into him.

"What's wrong?"

"Crud, I forgot. It's Ladies Day."

"I'm sure you're welcome," I said, taking his hand and tugging him inside.

The first thing I noticed was the store looked more like an exclusive boutique than a sex toy store. Will was right. There were quite a few ladies present. The amused female chatter was deafening.

Will cringe, and I giggled.

"You don't understand, my sister works here on Ladies Day," he grumbled.

I turned to look at him, startled. Not the blonde I'd mistaken for a rival, I hoped. "Which one?" I asked, tensing. Instead of answering, he peered over my shoulder.

"Too late."

Courtney strode over to us with a big grin on her expressive face, and I felt doubly embarrassed. First, I'd been jealous of her out on the street, and now, I was shopping for sex toys. But the sympathetic smile on the other woman's face made me forget my awkwardness.

"Introduce us, big brother," Courtney demanded.

Will let out a sigh of defeat, reluctantly stepping forward to make the introductions. "Courtney, this is April. April, this is my pesky kid sister, Courtney." His frown deepened. "By the way, I still don't approve of your job. You shouldn't be working in a place like this."

"A place like this," Monica said, stepping up to them. "I'll have you know, this is a high class establishment. All lingerie designed by yours truly and my trusty assistant, Courtney."

I grinned, gazing at Monica. She'd changed a lot from our school days. Gone was the skinny tomboy who'd favored scraggly brown pigtails. In her place was a voluptuous brunette with luxurious hair and a wicked twinkle in her green eyes.

"Hi, Modest Monica."

Monica's eyes widened. "Awesome April, is that really you?" she cried, reaching out to hug me.

I smiled. "It sure is. It's great to see you."

"I heard you were back in town, and I can see you're in good hands," she joked, looking at Will.

"You've got that right," I said, amused.

"Well, I'd better get back to work. We'll talk later."

"Okay," I said, watching her go.

"What are you doing here, brother dear?" Courtney teased. "Don't you know it's Ladies Day?"

He frowned. "That's what I was—"

"You here to buy him something for his birthday?" Courtney turned to ask me, interrupting him.

"Something special for his birthday. What a great idea! What would you like?" I asked, glancing at Will.

He was gazing around the room. His eyes lit up on the swing in the corner, the lingerie on display, then flitted to the red spanking paddle and blindfold on the table in front of us.

"Don't bother asking him. He's too busy drooling over the goodies. Typical man. Are you coming to dinner Friday?"

"Of course, I am. I wouldn't miss it for the world." I smiled.

"Good, I'm glad he bit the bullet and asked you."

I noted Will tensing at the mention of the family meal, and Courtney's intimation that it would be an ordeal. I remembered his mom from day camp. The lady had been a dynamo, practically running the summer program, and very friendly. How bad could it be? From his tense expression, it was obviously a sore point for him. I'd probably feel just as apprehensive if my dad sat Will down for a talk about his honorable intentions. Lucky for him, my parents were cruising the west coast in their RV, a favorite pastime in their retirement years.

I took his hand, gaining Will's attention from his sister. "Will, why don't you go? I'll find my own way home in about half an hour."

"I'll give her a ride," Courtney volunteered.

He nodded and drew me a distance away to say, "I'll leave you in good hands, then." He bent to give me a quick kiss. Pulling away, he smiled at me. "Have a good time, April, and buy something fun."

I watched him go, the bell chiming behind him. Then, I turned and looked at the goodies lining the shelves. This was the perfect place to buy his birthday present. Feeling like a kid in a candy store, I gazed at the exotic wares. I couldn't resist picking up the red paddle Will had stared at. It was bigger than a ping-pong paddle, and padded. I smacked it against my jean-clad thigh, and let out a giggle at the stinging heat. It gave her ideas. The whole store gave her ideas.

"Come on," Courtney said, walking up to me. "The fashion show is about to start."

I fell into step with her. "What kind of fashion show?"

"Beautiful lingerie designed by Monica and me. Not the cheesy stuff some other stores sell."

I sat in a folding chair. I was warmed by the fact I'd been welcomed so warmly by Courtney. My gaze kept sneaking back to the red thong panties and bra on the mannequin. Will had given them a lingering glance. I definitely had to have them.

"Now, ladies," Monica said, "Let's get this party rocking. Here's Angela modeling Midnight Lace."

I watched a brunette walk by in a black lace nightgown.

"Wow." It was another must buy for my new lingerie collection.

Friday evening, I accompanied Will to his parent's home for his birthday dinner. I only hoped that they all liked me. I knew he had two other siblings I hadn't met yet. If they were as friendly as Courtney and Matt, I already knew I was going to love them. His mom, I remembered, as a kindly, smiling lady. His dad was an unknown factor. I'd never met him.

Will pulled into the wide driveway of his parent's long rambling ranch style home. The house was painted a light blue and a riot of colorful annuals tumbled from its window boxes. The driveway was already full of cars. Will parked behind a tan minivan.

I felt a twinge of nervousness. Meeting so many Sheppards en mass was going to be a bit disconcerting. Will seemed to read my emotions, reaching across the truck's bench seat to touch my hand.

"You don't have to do this, precious. I can make your excuses."

I loved him for giving me an easy way out, but I couldn't take it. "Don't be silly. I'm fine. I'm looking forward to it."

He turned off the ignition, got out, and walked around to help me out of the truck. I clung to his hand on the walk up the driveway. How much scrutiny would I be under? It was too late to chicken out. I'd just have to hope for the best.

Instead of worrying, I decided to loosen up by thinking about tonight. I was wearing some of the scandalous new undies I'd bought at Spice under my aqua and cream sundress. The thong panties bared my bottom, making me feel naughty and excited. Will was going to get so hot and bothered when he saw them, I thought with a tremor of anticipation.

I'd spent a small fortune at the erotic boutique, but it was worth it. Saturday night, Will was going to have a birthday surprise he'd never forget. It was the least I could do to repay him for my new sexual liberation. Will never tired of teaching me love lessons, and I was an eager pupil.

His hand was warm on my back as he escorted me to the front door. He didn't bother to knock, just ushered me inside. I looked around the living room's homey décor, feeling a little more relaxed. Family photos perched atop an entertainment center and lined the walls. I grinned upon seeing one of Will as a gap-toothed young boy.

He took my elbow and steered me toward the kitchen where lively female voices could be heard chatting and joking. "We might as well get this over with." His step slowed and he added, "I probably should have warned you. Don't let anything my mom says bother you."

Warned me? What did he mean by that? What did he expect his mom to say that might bother me? I remembered his mother as a sweet lady, who made a mean s'more and could start a campfire with one match. How bad could she be?

Just then, I heard a cry of delight, and turned to find what had to be Will's mom bearing down on us. Slightly plump with ash blonde hair and sparkling brown eyes, she hadn't changed much since day camp. And she was smiling. I instantly relaxed.

"William, how nice to see you. We were starting to worry you weren't coming. Give your mom a hug." She enveloped him in a bear hug, then pulled back to smile at me. "And this must be April. I remember you as a little girl. All my little ones have grown up. I've heard a lot about you from Mathew. Welcome to the family, my dear."

"Thanks," I said, flustered as the woman embraced me, enveloping her in a cloud of Channel Number Five.

I peered at Will over his mom's shoulder. He was smiling, but I could see the tense set of his shoulders. He was worried about how I'd take the enthusiastic welcome. It was a bit disconcerting, a *welcome to the family*, just like that. His mother practically had us married off. Now I knew what he wanted to warn me about. I smiled at him, and he relaxed. When his mom let go and stepped back, I took a deep breath, mentally putting on the brakes.

"Well, aren't you going to introduce us, William?" his mother demanded, hands on her hips.

William? I couldn't help sliding a teasing grin his way.

His eyes twinkled back at me. "Mother, this is April Brooks, as you well know. April, this is my mother, Cynthia Shepard."

Cynthia nodded, taking my arm and towing me toward the kitchen table where Will's dad sat. "Come and meet William's dad. My son is a chip off the old block, wouldn't you say?"

I would have recognized Will's father anywhere. He was an older, heavier, dead ringer for Will, right down to the dark hair and blue eyes.

"You're right," I said to Will's mom.

Cynthia's eyes twinkled as she said, "They've both got the same Shepard stubborn streak a mile wide, but I imagine you've found that out already."

I laughed. "You've got that one right. I'll have to ask you for tips on handling a Shepard male sometime."

Earl stood as we neared the table. "You must be April. I'm glad to meet you, young lady."

"Same here," I said with a grin as he pumped my hand.

"Take it easy, Earl," Will's mom scolded. "You'll bruise the poor girl."

I held back a chuckle as Will's father let go of my hand with a rueful smile. It took a strong woman to handle these Shepard males.

I smiled. "Don't worry, sir, I'm stronger than I look."

"I'll vouch for that," Will said with a pleased chuckle, putting a hand on my shoulder.

I leaned into his touch like a flower to sunlight, my move instinctive.

Will's parents exchanged a pleased look. They seemed to approve, making me feel so much better.

Earl nodded. "Well, I'd better get out to the grill before Mathew burns the steaks. William, why don't you come help me?"

He went out the patio door onto the flagstone patio where Matt and two other men stood telling stories by a smoking grill. Behind them, several children played on the swing set.

"Okay, Dad." Will said, and then turned to me, taking my hand. "You sure you're okay here, precious?"

I squeezed his hand and let it go. "I'm fine. Go have some guy talk with your dad and brothers."

He gave me a smile.

I watched him walk out to the patio and accept a beer from Matt, with a laugh at something his brother said. Will's mom touched my arm, gaining my attention.

I turned to look at her indulgent smile, knowing that my heart was on my sleeve. My feelings for Will were obviously visible to the other woman.

Cynthia smiled. "Won't you come into the kitchen and meet the girls? I believe you've already met Courtney."

I followed her into the kitchen. I smiled at Courtney tossing a salad. A tall brunette, who I pegged for Will's older sister, Meg, was at the stove stirring something spicy. The pregnant blonde pulling jars of condiments out of the refrigerator had to be Lance's wife, Jane.

"Everyone," Wills mother said. "This is April, Will's girl."

I felt a little spark of delight at the title. "Hi."

The pregnant blonde shut the refrigerator door, carrying a jar of pickles to the counter. "Hi. I'm Jane, Lance's wife."

"She's due to have our third grandchild any day now," Will's mom put in.

"Yup," Jane agreed with a grin. "I'm a week overdue and just about to pop."

"And I'm Will's older sister, Meg. It's nice to meet you, April." She smiled at me as she put a lid on her saucepan, and then turned to her sister-in-law. "Eat some of my chili sauce on your steak, Jamey dear, and it might just solve your problem."

Jane giggled, and everyone erupted into laughter. After a moment, Will's mom shushed them with a smile. "Quiet, girls, we don't want to make April think we're given to coarse language."

"Yes, Mom," Meg said with a smile.

"Don't you worry, Mrs. Shepard, I think you're all wonderful. Hello, everybody. Thanks for the warm welcome," I replied, touched by the cheery greeting. I didn't know what Will was worried about. We were getting along famously.

"Come, let's get better acquainted," Will's mom said, steering me toward the stools at the end of the eat-in counter.

I perched on the stool, reminding me of the night I'd met Will at Red's, and prepared myself for the interrogation.

"So, tell me about yourself, April," Cynthia said with a friendly smile, while gazing intently at me.

Knowing I was being judged, I tried to stay relaxed. I smiled, saying softly, "Well, Mrs. Shepard, as you know, I was born and raised here. I went to school here and I collected more badges than anyone else at day camp."

"I remember," she said with a smile. "How are your parents?"

"Fine. After Dad retired from the paper, they brought an RV, and are having a ball traveling around the country."

"That's nice to hear," she said with a smile, then sobered. "Tell me a little about your life after you left home."

I knew she was asking about other men, without actually saying the words. I tried to sidestep the issue, embarrassed. "I worked as an Assistant Professor of Biology for several years at the university. After my Aunt Sadie had her stroke, I came home to run The Rosebud." She sighed.

"Yes, how is dear Sadie?"

"She's improving, slowly. It'll take months of rehab to regain her skills, and when she does, she won't be able to run the inn. She sold it to me."

"And William and Mathew are doing your renovations?"

"That's right. He's renovating me," I murmured. In more ways than one, I thought cheekily.

The twinkle in the lady's eyes told me she got it, and she approved.

"What about your personal life, April dear? Any other men on the horizon?"

The woman wasn't easily diverted.

"There was someone, but we broke up before I moved home." I noticed a small flare of concern in her eyes. "I promise you, it's over. Will knows all about it, and understands." I hurried to add, "Your son means too much to me to even try to deceive him."

Will's mother nodded. "Good. It's refreshing to find a young woman with your moral character. You are a breath of fresh air," Cynthia said with a warm chuckle. "You're just what the doctor ordered to make my son happy again."

"Thanks," I said, wondering what she was getting at. It was news to me that Will had been unhappy before I came on the scene. Why? Had some other woman tromped on his heart?

That could explain his anger when he thought I didn't trust him. I'd ask him about it tonight.

When we got back to the inn, I led Will to my bedroom. "Have a seat," I said.

He dropped into a bedside chair, eyeing me speculatively.

I waited a moment, then started my little striptease, putting on a private show for my man. Unbuttoning the row of small pearl buttons down the front of my sundress, I flashed him a coquettish smile. Hearing his breathing grow fast, I slowly opened the bodice, then turned my back on him, making him wait as I gradually let my dress drop to the floor.

"Oops," I said, stepping to the side, bending to pick up the dress, letting my bare bottom in red thong panties curve teasingly at him.

His breathing grew ragged behind me, and I was glad I'd bought new undies. Turning back to face him, I cupped my breasts in the red bra, pushing them up so they almost tumbled out, the edges of my nipples exposed. His eyes darkened, and the arousal on his face made my knees weak.

"Come here, April," he demanded.

I shook my head, teasing him, rubbing my fingers over my nipples. They budded tight in response. The outrage flaring in his eyes excited me.

"Make me," I said with a nervous giggle.

In a flash, he snagged my arm, tugging me into his grasp. Sprawling against him, off balance, I could only whimper when he reached up to stroke my tingling nipples though the lacy bra.

"Such pretty tits," he growled, rolling the nipples hard between his fingers. "It's not nice to tease your man that way."

"Maybe I don't want to be nice." Flashing a wicked smile at him, I murmured, "Sometimes, a little teasing is nice."

"You think so, do you?" His mouth latched onto one of my nipples through the fabric.

I groaned as he sucked hard, drawing my nipple deep into his mouth, and I collapsed onto his lap. He didn't miss a beat. He kept sucking. Then, his hand found my mound over my panties. He pressed the fabric into the cleft of my pussy.

Moving to suck my other nipple, he growled. "I love your new panties, precious. Very erotic, like you."

He thought I was erotic? How wonderful. I felt erotic with him.

His cock was growing under me. I could feel it pulsing under my thighs, under the hot mound of my pussy.

My hand snaked down to his pants. "I want you, Will."

Suddenly, he stood up, and I let out a cry of protest. Swatting my bottom, he bent me over the arm of the chair.

Shocked and excited, I gasped when his hot lips skimmed down my spine. Trembling, I felt him kneel behind me to kiss the globes of my buttocks.

"I want you," I moaned, aching for him.

"Patience," he said, nibbling on my bottom, first one cheek, and then the other. Making love bites, teasing me.

I was on fire, a heat wave rushing through me as my pussy clenched.

"Oh," I gasped when he nipped me harder.

He pulled down my panties, and his talented tongue flicked at my pussy from behind. I arched my back, whimpering at the pleasure. He flicked his tongue around my anus, and my knees wobbled. I groaned, shuddering, as he moved back to tease my pussy.

"Please, I need you."

He stood, and I heard his zipper. His cock butted against my bottom before he slipped into my pussy.

I groaned, contracting around his shaft as he leaned over me, his hands cupping my breasts. Teasing my aching nipples, he pumped into me, his balls slapping me with each thrust, adding to my pleasure. Lifting my upper body up, he brought me down on this thrusting cock, impaling me.

"Yes. Yes," I cried, rippling.

With one hard thrust, he pinched my nipples, and I saw stars behind my closed eyes, convulsing in an overwhelming orgasm.

He held me tight as he came.

The phone rang moments later, pulling me out of my afterglow.

I cast a reluctant glance at the jangling bedside phone.

"Let the machine pick up," he said, setting me back on my feet and steadying me. He reached for my robe, handing it to me.

I belted the terrycloth robe around my middle.

We were both probably thinking the same thing. This might be another obscene phone call. After what he and I had been doing, it almost made me feel tawdry.

He rubbed my arm. "Don't think that, precious. It's not the same thing."

I wasn't surprised he'd picked up on my thoughts. We were on the same wavelength in so many ways.

After several more rings, the answering machine light came on.

"Got 'em," Will said, striding toward the phone. He pushed the play button, and heavy breathing echoed in the bedroom.

I rubbed my arms, feeling chilled, despite the fluffy robe I was wearing. "That's him," I acknowledged.

He took my hand and drew me toward the phone. "Do you recognize the number?"

"No." I glanced at the unfamiliar digits. "The area code is from the southeast part of the state, where I used to live." I glanced Will's way. He was frowning, his stance stiff like he was ready for battle. "You don't think it could be Edmund, do you?"

"That'd be my guess," he said in a low grumble. "I'll kill that jerk."

"Don't you know violence never solved anything?"

His tight scowl told me he didn't agree. He'd like nothing better than to punch Edmund out for all his misdeeds. While I appreciated the thought, I knew now my ex simply wasn't worth the effort. I knew a worthy man when I saw one, and he was standing right in front of me.

I took his hand, leading him away from the phone and back toward the chair we'd made love on. Giving him a little push, I had him ease down into the chair, and slipping onto his lap, said, "First of all, we don't even know for sure Edmund's the culprit. That wasn't his phone number. Second, we'll turn the number and message over to your friend at the police station." Feeling his tension ebb, I smiled at him. "You and I can think of a much more pleasurable way to spend the night than worrying about that turkey."

CHAPTER 8

Saturday, I walked into Red's by Will's side. It was his birthday, and we were going to celebrate with the members of his crew. I had a private celebration of my own planned back at the inn.

Tingling, I blushed when I imagined his reaction to my gift. Who would have thought things would have turned out this way? Three weeks ago, I'd been a timid virgin, looking for someone to deflower me. Now, I was a sexual wanton, having a torrid affair with a hunk that made me melt with his touch and cream my panties with a look.

"Ready, precious?" Will asked as we neared the door.

"Yes." I smiled at him.

The jukebox was blaring, as usual. He opened the door and escorted me inside.

"Matt's got a table reserved in back," Will shouted in my ear to be heard over the din.

"Okay." I started moving, his hand pressing my back, stopping here and there when Will paused to greet friends.

He was very popular in the community, I realized, and with the ladies, too. A few were giving him the eye. To his credit, he didn't look back. A one-woman man. I liked that in him. I glowed with pride.

We finally made our way to the back booths. Matt occupied the one I'd been sitting in that first night I'd met Will. How funny. Will's grin told her he remembered, too.

"You two lovebirds finally made it," Matt said. "Greg and Brandi are playing a little pool." He gestured to the couple bent over the pool table.

"Greg runs Baker's Hardware," Will said into my ear. "Brandi's his wife. The other couple is Ron Cotter, he's been renovating your plumbing system, and his fiancée, Janet."

"Right," I said. I recognized Ron as one of Will's subcontractors. "Hi," I said when he nodded between shots.

"I thought this was a couple's party." Will teased Matt, asking, "Couldn't you find a date?"

"Told you before, I'm having too much fun playing the field."

Matt winked at a passing waitress, and I figured he scored all the time. Did Will miss playing the field? His relaxed smile, and his hand rubbing my knee under the table, told me no.

I sipped my beer, feeling more at home, looking forward to later, when a sultry blonde breezed by. Will went stone still, his eyes following the overly made-up woman in the tight red dress. Out of the corner of my eye, I watched Matt scowl at the blonde, too. Her curious glance at Will brought grim-faced silence.

Who the heck was she to have the brothers so on edge? I had to know. When Brandi and Greg came to the table, I smiled at her. Brandi was bound to be a good source of information.

"I'm going to the powder room, want to tag along?" I got up and walked away with Brandi trailing behind me.

Once inside the ladies' room, I looked around to make sure we were alone, then turned to Brandi, who was putting on fresh lipstick in front of the mirror.

"Who is she?"

Brandi turned a startled gaze my way. "You mean, you don't know?"

"No. I don't know. Who is she?" I asked calmly, not wanting to overreact again.

"Tammy Edwards, his ex."

My jaw dropped. "Ex-girlfriend?"

"No, his ex-wife." Brandi bit her lip. "Sorry."

I gulped, not knowing how to react to the startling information. Will had been angry when I didn't tell him about my ex-fiancé. Now, to find out he had a broken marriage behind him, astounded me. But it did explain his mother's assertion that he'd been hurt by someone.

Brandi nodded. "They've been divorced for two years. She screwed around on him, and dumped him for a dentist from another town. A guy with more money. Looks like she's back, and take it from me, she's trouble."

I felt my spirit crumbling. "What if he never got over her?"

"I doubt it. He said he was well rid of her. And, he's been skittish around women, until you, that is. You're his first steady partner since."

As the powder room door opened, Brandi fell silent, then murmured, "Speak of the devil."

I turned to find the other woman standing there. Tammy's thick makeup might have made her look like a painted doll, if it weren't for the sour scowl. Her tight red dress left little to the imagination clinging to her thin body and obviously surgically enhanced breasts. They stood out on her chest like two balls.

She looked me up and down scornfully. "Frankly, I don't know what he sees in you."

Stung by the catty comment, I glared back at her. "Ditto," I said with a defiant grin, mimicking Will's speech. "But in your case, *saw* would be the operative word. I don't know what he *saw* in you."

"Slut." Her eyes narrowed. "That's funny, coming from the likes of you. Why don't you go back to your fiancé at the college, teacher?"

I blinked at her, stunned. How did she know about Edmund? The woman had dug up dirt on me for a purpose? To worm her way back into Will's life? No way!

"Why don't you go back to your husband, the dentist? Or did he dump you, too?" At the woman's glower, I knew I'd hit on the truth. "Doesn't feel so good, does it?"

"Bitch!" Tammy yelled, turning on her heel and tearing out of the ladies' room.

"Bravo," Brandi said, clapping me on the back.

I took a calming breath. "Come on. I've got to go rescue Will from her clutches." I pulled open the door and ran headlong into him.

Will's arms came around to steady me when I bounced off of him.

"You okay, precious?" he asked.

I gazed at the troubled look in his eyes, and gave him a reassuring smile. "I'm fine. How about you?"

"I'll live. What did she say to you?" He cast an angry look at Tammy, who was nursing a drink at the far end of the bar.

"Enough. Don't worry, I handled her."

"She sure did," Brandi said with a grin. "Never saw anything like it. You've got yourself a keeper there, Will." She chuckled, slipping by them to head to the booth.

Will grabbed my hand. "Come on, we're outta here."

I followed him toward the front, noticing Tammy was now chatting up the man sitting on the bar stool next to her. The woman's harsh glare followed us to the door. I pretended not to notice.

When we got in the truck, I turned to Will. "Tell me about it."

He tilted his head, studying me in the parking lot light. "What do you want to know?"

"Everything, full disclosure." I softly smiled, trying to show him I wasn't jumping to the wrong conclusion.

"She comes back to town about every six months or so, usually between men, aiming to cause trouble."

"She wants you back," I said, trying not to sound jealous.

He pinned me with a serious gaze. "Doesn't matter, I don't want her. All I want is you, April."

I smiled. "Let's go home, cowboy."

He slipped the truck into gear and drove us back to The Rosebud. I tingled with anticipation. When the truck stopped, I hopped out and walked around the truck to take Will's hand.

"Come with me," I said, leading him toward the barn. It hadn't held horses for years, but I'd had it specially outfitted for tonight.

"What's up?" he asked, looking at me quizzically in the moonlight.

"You, I hope," I said with a flirty grin. "Your birthday present's in the barn. I want to give it to you."

He squeezed my hand. "What is it, a horse or something?"

"Well, it does have to do with riding. But that's your last clue, birthday boy. You'll have to wait and see."

He let out a low chuckle. "You're full of surprises tonight, April."

I smiled back at him, tugging his hand. "Stop dawdling and come on."

I opened the barn door, and pulled him inside, shutting it behind me, enclosing us in darkness.

"Are we going to play blind man's bluff?" he joked.

"You'll find out, cowboy." I switched on the light and stepped back, watching his stunned expression as he looked at the setup.

The barn had been completely cleaned, and I'd had bales of fresh hay placed strategically here and there. There was a hay pile for us to roll in, a feather bed to lay on, and a rocking horse with a saddle for us to have sex. I'd even rigged a sex swing at the proper height, in case he wanted to take me that way.

I plopped a Stetson on his head. "Ride 'em, cowboy."

He grinned. His fevered gaze scanned the barn, settling on me. "It's just what I wanted," he husked, closing the distance between us. "I can't wait to unwrap my gift."

He peeled off my shirt and bra while he kissed me. I shivered, excited, as his hands brushed over my bare breasts and tweaked my tingling nipples. He pulled down my pants and panties in one fell swoop. I stepped out of them and my shoes.

Naked, I sashayed across the barn, Will trailing after me.

Stopping by a table equipped with all the sensual supplies I could buy at Spice, I waved my hand over the array. Lotions, lubricants, a vibrator, a blindfold, handcuffs, and the red spanking paddle he'd looked at lay there waiting to be used.

"What'll it be, cowboy?" I asked with a cheeky grin. Brushing my bare breasts against him, I said, my voice a soft bedroom purr, "I'm here to serve you all night long. Your wish is my command, birthday boy. No holds barred." Chuckling I added, "You're the master, and I'm your little sex kitten."

His irises contracted and the pulse throbbed in his throat. He just stood there, studying me for a moment, a fevered gleam in his eyes, making me hotter.

"The swing," he said, gruffly.

Grinning, I walked over to it.

His hands spanned my waist as he lifted me onto the seat. I gasped when my wet pussy plopped onto the hard seat, starved for him. My legs splayed lewdly open on the wide seat.

Will just stared at my exposed pussy for a hot moment. It got wetter, contracting.

Grasping the handles of the swing, he pulled me to him, kissing me passionately, his tongue surging inside my mouth when I opened for him.

I whimpered, rubbing my tingling nipples against his hard chest, wanting to hurry him.

He stopped the kiss, steadied the swing, and unzipped his jeans.

"I love my present," he growled, stepping between my splayed legs, swinging me close to him as he entered me. Gripping the edges of the swing's seat, he swung me away a little and then pulled me back to him, thrusting deeper.

I gasped, my pussy rippling on his cock as he swung me. Gazing deep into the fiery gleam of his blue eyes, I moaned and held on tight for the ride of my life. Pulsating, I closed my eyes and gasped as he swung me faster, controlling the pace.

"Come," he demanded, thrusting hard, and holding me tightly to him, buried deep inside me.

I convulsed with a tight spasm. I came, him jerking and pumping inside me.

I opened my eyes. He was looking at me with a sexy smile.

"Did I mention that I love my present?"

"Once or twice," I said with a satisfied grin.

He pulled away, and helped me off the swing. My knees were a bit wobbly, and he held me up while I got my bearings.

"Time for some cowboy treats," I said, leading him toward the hamper.

"Red eye chili and beans?" he asked, chuckling.

"No, champagne and birthday cake." I handed him the bottle to open, and then lit the candles on the chocolate birthday cake I'd baked. I looked at him. "Blow out the candles and make a wish."

He popped the cork on the champagne. "It's already come true, precious." He leaned forward to kiss me, pressing the cold bottle against my breasts.

I gasped into his mouth at the stinging pleasure, my nipples beading. When he pulled away, I caught a knowing grin on his face, and blushed. He had lots more to teach me.

He blew out his candles, and I served him his cake, nibbling at a piece.

"This is the best cake I've ever tasted," he praised.

"Better not tell your momma that," I said with a chuckle.

Getting an idea, I knelt in front of him. Trickling champagne onto his cock, I slipped his semi-hard penis into my hot mouth, and sucked on it. He pulsed between my lips, growing hot and stiff.

Pulling away, I looked up at him and smiled. "What next, cowboy?"

"The handcuffs and blindfold," he said with a wicked twinkle in his eyes. "It's time for a birthday spanking."

I shivered, feeling a zing of mingled apprehension and excitement. I'd thought twice about setting up the bondage and discipline supplies, but I was excited about it, too. I'd even read some erotic romances dealing with domestic discipline, so I was prepared to role play.

I stood and walked to the table, waiting for him. There was a look of tense anticipation on his face. I held my wrists up for him to shackle.

"You are the hottest woman on earth," he said, kissing me as he clicked the cuffs on my wrists.

I smiled, trying not to be nervous. My pussy was wet and spasmodic, my nipples hard with excitement, and my bottom tightened. How much would it hurt? When he picked up the blindfold and slipped it over my eyes, plunging me into darkness, my pulse raced. This was a little scary.

His hot lips slanted over mine, and I pressed my naked body against him, moaning with excitement as his tongue surged into my mouth. His hands roved over me, sliding down my back to cup my bottom, pinching my cheeks erotically. I gasped, shocked, and heard him chuckle. Then, his hands moved up to cup my breasts, his rough fingers fanning over the nipples, making them harder, tingling. I felt a tugging deep inside my body. He pinched them harder, and I gasped at the pleasure/pain.

"Oh my," I murmured when he broke the kiss.

He grasped my arm. "Come with me, precious."

I walked blindly beside him, trusting him not to lead me into danger. When he drew me to a halt, my middle brushed against leather. The saddle, I realized. He was going to bend me over it and spank me—how scandalous. My pussy fluttered and I quivered deep inside, suddenly nervous.

"Don't worry, precious. The spanking won't be too hard, but I sure as hell will be."

I shivered at the words, excited and a little scared, but I trusted him. He kissed my shoulder. My tummy and pubic bone made contact with the saddle as he bent me over it, moving forward to hook my cuffs over a peg. Stretched out and exposed, I was embarrassed and turned-on beyond belief.

"Five spanks, I think," he said, rubbing my bottom teasingly with the paddle.

"Okay," I said a bit tremulously.

I yelped when it made stinging contact with my bottom.

"Oh." It stung, but didn't hurt. Tears misted my eyes behind my blindfold and my pussy convulsed.

Swat.

I bit my lip, my hips grinding against the saddle.

Swat.

"Oh." It stung more, my pussy quivered, getting hotter and wetter.

Swat.

I ground against the saddle, stifling a moan as pleasure and pain overwhelmed my senses.

Swat.

I yelped, butt stinging as he made the last one harder.

Aroused and embarrassed, I was glad I was wearing the blindfold. My pussy was soaked, creamy with excitement, while my bottom burned and throbbed a bit. I was so turned on.

His hands cupped and caressed my punished ass cheeks, his finger probing into my anus. "Was it a good spanking, precious?"

"Yes," I moaned, almost humping his hand.

"I want to fuck you back here, my cock up your ass. Would you let me?"

I inhaled, tightening around his finger. I suddenly craved to be taken that way.

"That's why I bought the lube. Ride me, cowboy."

He stepped away, then returned to spread cool lubricant around and inside me, and I pushed back at him. Having his finger and tongue there was so sexy, but what about his cock?

His cock touched me, rock hard and hot, and he pushed just a little bit inside.

I gasped, startled by the initial pain. It burned and stretched.

"Easy, babe," he said with a groan, stilling, letting me adjust to him.

I forcibly relaxed, the pain easing, to be replaced by hunger.

He pressed into me a millimeter at a time, making little groans deep in his throat. The sound turned me on almost as much as his cock invading. My face was flaming behind the blindfold. My whole body was on fire. He inched further inside me, and pleasure/pain assaulted me. It hurt. It felt good. I whimpered, clenching around him. He was so hot and big. Could I hold him? With a final gentle thrust, he buried himself to the hilt.

I gasped, impaled, as he rested against my hot paddled bottom. My body clutched at his cock as I adjusted to him.

A wave of sensual pleasure started to flow though me, while he lay motionless inside me. My whole bottom half was gripping him, tugging at his cock, and I yearned for him to move, to take me somewhere I hadn't been before, despite the ache.

He groaned and started to move, slowly at first, and then faster, deeper. Crying out as waves of pleasure and pain quivered through me, I arched my spine, taking all he had to give.

He groaned, rocking into me hard, his balls slapping.

My body tightening, I moaned as a fierce wave of orgasm took me. My ass milking at his cock, I came, sagging against the saddle, my knees buckling.

He pushed into me one last time and came, spurting deep inside me. He pressed tight to me as my little after-spasms tugged at both of us.

He kissed my shoulder, still buried inside me. "Thank you for making my fantasies come true, April. You are my fantasy girl."

I smiled, sandwiched between the saddle and him. "And you, cowboy, are my fantasy man. Who would have thought being spanked could make me so turned-on?"

He chuckled. "I didn't hurt you, did I?"

"Let's put it this way, I should still be able to sit down tomorrow."

"I can't believe you went to all this trouble for my birthday."

"Anything for you, cowboy."

CHAPTER 9

I went into town for supplies. The renovations were almost complete at The Rosebud and I wanted to make a celebration dinner. Later, I was going to take Will out to the barn and ravish him all over again. *Ride me cowboy,* indeed. I was fast becoming insatiable for him.

But what I felt for him went way beyond lust. I loved him. It was just that simple. A special man, he had a way of making me feel safe, cherished, and adventurous all at the same time. And while Will had never said the three little words 'I love you', I knew that he cared.

Neither one of us had talked about continuing our affair after the renovations were through, but I wanted to. And somehow, I trusted he felt the same. It was an unspoken understanding, but I wanted more. I was going to broach the subject tonight right after dinner.

Going into the store, I bought thick steaks and all the fixings for dinner. Man food. Will would need his strength for the special sexual tryst I had planned for the night. I picked up some ginseng tea for stamina, then strolled by the ice cream aisle, picking up chocolate syrup and whipped cream.

I was heading for the checkout stand when my cart was hit hard from the side.

Letting out a startled squeak, I looked at the person who'd bumped me. Will's ex-wife Tammy stood there glaring at me. The woman had deliberately rammed my cart. Was she completely nuts?

Tammy scowled. "Why don't you go back where you belong, schoolteacher?"

"I could ask you the same thing." I grabbed Tammy's arm, earning a gasp of alarm from the woman, and dragged her off to a side aisle. "Okay, spill it, Tammy. What do you want?"

"Well, I, um," she stammered, looking down. "My husband, of course."

I caught the startled look on the woman's face, the guilty flush under her makeup. Will was right, she thrived on chaos. She hadn't expected to be directly challenged. Whatever was behind it, I wasn't stepping aside for the slut—no way in hell.

"I don't think so. You just want to cause trouble for him." Staring down the other woman, I had the pleasure of seeing her blink in confused surprise.

Tammy scowled, her lips thinning. She turned and stomped away, muttering, "Told him it wouldn't work."

I watched her go with mingled feelings of relief and confusion. *Told who it wouldn't work? Had she made an end run and already approached Will? Another question to pose tonight.*

After I checked out, I walked to the parking lot, keeping a wary eye out for the nut, but didn't see her. Relieved, I headed back home.

Pulling into the driveway, I noticed Will and his crew's vehicles were still here. Will was probably working on his secret project in my bedroom. We'd been sleeping at his place for the past week. He'd banned me from my bedroom, making me crazy to find out what he was working on. But I'd controlled my curiosity and hadn't peeked. When he showed it to me, I'd be properly surprised.

I took a parking spot next to the barn. Turning off the engine, I turned to grab the whipped cream and chocolate syrup out of the grocery bag, and got out of the car. I'd use them to ravish Will tonight. I carried them into the barn and headed for the mini fridge he had insisted on installing the morning after his birthday orgy.

Tonight, I planned to turn Will into my own private man-sized chocolate sundae. Tingling at the thought, I put them into the fridge next to some of our favorite nibbles and a bottle of bubbly. A midnight snack and a night of bliss, what more could a girl ask for?

Shutting the fridge door and standing, I was shocked to see Edmund standing in the open doorway.

Tall and thin with sandy hair and light blue eyes, he was wearing one of his favorite tweed suits with leather patches sewn on the elbows. Trying to look the part of a professor was just one of his affectations, I realized. As he advanced on me, the barn door ajar behind him, I went instantly on edge. I backed away. "Edmund, what are you doing here?"

He ignored my question, brushing a bit of hay off his impeccably clean jacket while he glanced around the barn. Seemingly fascinated, he gazed at the swing, saddle, and feather bed for a long moment, then turned to ask, "What goes on in here, April dearest?"

"One guess," I said, resenting the pet name as his suddenly heated gaze flicked back to me. Good grief, the set up was turning the jerk on. I openly scowled back at him, not caring what he thought of me.

His eyes narrowed, his expression soured. "I never knew you were such a little slut. Maybe my phone calls heated you up."

The disclosure didn't come as a surprise. The police had tracked my harassing calls back to a pay phone on campus about two weeks ago. "So, you were the one making those disgusting phone calls."

"Of course, who else would bother?" he said in a distracted tone, seeming to lose interest in me. Stepping up to the table, he gazed at the array of items and picked up the handcuffs, fingering them. He looked at me with a speculative expression in his icy eyes.

My sense of outrage boiled over at seeing him handling Will's toys. "Take your hands off my lover's property."

Edmund shook his head. "Correction, he's not yours. He's got a wife who's come to claim him, just like I've come to claim you." His eyes glittered with interest. "Come here, April, and show me what you've learned."

I backed away, appalled. How could he even suggest such a thing, or think I'd go along with it? I scowled at him. "Why should I? You definitely don't have the equipment it would take."

His hand tightened on the handcuffs, his knuckles turning white. He threw me a venomous glare. "Why, you ungrateful little bitch. I ought to—"

"You ass, you're the one who got Will's ex-wife riled up."

He was obviously furious at having his shortcomings mentioned. His eyes were practically bugged out. He'd started it, and I'd fight fire with fire if I had to. His mention of Will's ex-wife told the tale. He knew he didn't have what it took to get me back, so he was counting on tricks and outside forces to send me running back to him. It wasn't going to work.

"It didn't take much. The woman's highly unstable. She's liable to go after you with a hatchet if you don't wise up," he threatened in a clipped voice, dropping the handcuffs.

I didn't even blink. It was an idle threat, and I knew it. "For your information, she and I already had it out at the grocery store, and she blinked. I suspect she's already on her way out of town, and I suggest you follow her before I call the law. There's already a record of your harassing calls, and it wouldn't take much to get you thrown in jail."

"No," he said through a sigh, his stance softening as he stuffed his hands in his pockets. "I can't walk away, April. I need you."

"Yeah, right." I scowled. I wasn't buying his suddenly harmless, contrite pose, either. The man should have gone on the stage. He'd have made a hell of an actor. "Why don't you go pick on Tiffany?"

"Tiff and I are though. It's you I love, dearest."

I crossed my arms, chilled. Why couldn't he take a hint from my negative tone and walk away? "I don't believe that for a second. Anyway, I certainly don't love you. In fact, I don't know what I ever saw in you."

His thin lips tightened. "All right, have it your way. Dean Moreland is ready to fire my ass unless I finish those articles you were working on."

So, that was his motivation for this desperate attempt to get me back. I could see the desperation in his eyes, hear it in his clipped tone. It hurt his pride to admit the truth. He simply couldn't hack it academically without a dupe to back him up.

I shrugged, not giving a damn. He could sink or swim on his own merits. "That's your problem, Edmund. Write them yourself."

"You know I've got writer's block. Forget all this foolishness, and come back to the university. Your position is still open.

I intercepted your resignation letter, and told them you were taking a sabbatical instead."

I stared at him aghast. He had to have snagged my letter once it got to the administration building. But, why? *To keep me as his unwitting dupe*, came the answer.

"How dare you." His devious actions boggled my mind.

"Sorry. I knew you were overwrought after my sexual lapse, and I wanted to give you time to change your mind." Hanging his head, he added, "Even if you don't want to come back to me, I'll pay you to finish them."

I wrinkled my nose, hearing the false note of humility in his plea. What a fool I'd been, writing the articles that had gotten him published in scientific journals, while he took credit for them. There'd probably been a long line of women before me who had done the same thing for him, not that I gave a fig anymore.

Whether Edmund Jones was stupid or lazy, I didn't know, and I didn't care. He was still trying to play me for a fool. No more!

"Again," I said slowly. "That's your problem, Edmund. I'm not coming back."

He looked up at me then, his eyes narrowed with rage again. I watched his thin lips twitch, his fists ball at his sides. He stalked toward me, and I knew I was in trouble.

Suddenly realizing how out of control he was, I backed away. With all the sawing and hammering in the house, who'd hear me scream? Bumping into the saddle, I grabbed the paddle hanging on the pommel.

Holding it in front of me, I warned, "Stay away from me, Edmund, or I'll hurt you."

He laughed. "You think that's going to stop me?"

"No, but this will." I lobbed it at him hard, bouncing it off his nose.

Howling, he grabbed his nose as blood spurted.

The barn door jerked wide open, and Will filled the doorway. "What in the hell's going on in here?"

I ran to him, trembling. "It's Edmund, he's crazy. He was trying to make me go back with him."

Will pushed me behind him and advanced on Edmund.

Edmund glared. "So, this hulking brute is your lover? Messing around with cowboys, how low can you get, April?"

I took a step toward him. How dare he cast aspersions on Will's blue-collar roots? At least he made an honest dollar. "Why you—"

"Easy, precious," Will said, blocking my path.

Edmund wiped his bloody nose. "She's my fiancée, and she's out of control. I've come to take her back."

Will adopted a loose stance, clearly ready for battle, and I shivered.

"I'm not your anything anymore. Go away, Edmund."

"You heard the lady," Will said flatly. "She's doesn't want you in her life anymore. Beat it."

Edmund glared at me over Will's shoulder. "That bitch injured me. I'm going to sue her for every penny this tumbledown inn is worth, and then I'll go after your construction company. You won't be worth a dime when I get through with you. We'll see if she wants you then."

"Listen up!" Will shouted. "You've got two choices. Walk out or be carried out. The choice is yours."

"And, Edmund, try and sue either of us, and I'll get the board of regents on your butt. They'd love to know who really wrote those articles. And I kept excellent notes. I have all the documentation I need to hang you."

Edmund's jaw tightened as he glared at me. "You wouldn't do that to me."

Yeah, the old me wouldn't have, but the new woman I'd become in Will's arms definitely would. "Try me," I said in a calm, clear voice.

He paled, giving me a shocked once over. "Fine, there are lots of better qualified women who would love your old position." He gave us both a wide berth as he hightailed it out of the barn.

"Why don't you try Tiffany?" I yelled after him. "She was pretty good in a certain position from what I saw."

Will chuckled. "Well said, precious."

I listened to Edmund's ignition grind as he started his car, his tires squealing as he tore out of the driveway and sped away.

My tension didn't totally dissolve until Will came up behind me to rub my shoulders.

"Thank goodness, he's gone," I said, leaning into his strength.

"After what you said, I doubt he'll bother us again." Will turned me around and smiled. "Nicely done, precious."

"You, too. You're my hero, cowboy," I said, falling into his arms, trembling in a delayed reaction.

"Ditto," Will murmured, bending down to kiss me.

I sighed, my arms wrapping around his neck as he kissed me. The last remnants of fear vaporized as his tongue slipped into my mouth and his hands slid down my back to cup my bottom, pulling me to him.

He broke the kiss to nibble my ear, whispering, "You were magnificent, precious."

That evening, I laid Will out on the featherbed, teasing him. My bare breasts brushed against him as I manacled his wrists. He sucked on my nipple, making me gasp as I moved out of range. His body stretched taut, his cock already stirring, he was a hunk waiting to be ravished. This time, he was the one wearing the blindfold and handcuffs. I let out a delighted giggle.

"I'm at your mercy, precious," he said with a dry chuckle, flexing against his bonds as he teasingly rubbed against me. "Ravish away."

I bent to kiss him, brushing his sensual mouth with mine. I sucked at his lower lip, hearing him groan, then thrust my tongue into his mouth, rubbing my hard nipples against his chest. His breathing grew ragged.

Breaking the kiss and drawing away, I smiled at his groan of protest before I leaned forward to pop one plump nipple into his mouth. He groaned, sucking hard.

I whimpered. My knees went weak as he drew hard on my aching nipple. I moved so he could suck the other one while I slid my hand over his chest and abs. Pulling my nipple from his mouth, I moved lower, climbing onto the featherbed. Taking his hard cock in my hand, I straddled his head.

He licked my pussy, making me gasp as I drizzled chocolate sauce on his cock and sprayed whipped cream on it. I proceeded to lick it off, slurping and sucking, drawing his hot cock into my mouth. Bobbing up and down on his pulsing shaft, I whimpered as he pleasured me with his tongue, flicking at my clit.

Cupping his balls, I felt him tighten, about to come, and moved away. I wanted it to happen inside me.

Pulling away from his tantalizing tongue, I turned and straddled him, gasping as my pussy took his rampant cock. Fully inside me, I rocked, moaning at the waves of pleasure rippling through me.

Pulsating, I clamped around his cock, coming, as I cried out "I love you."

"Ditto, precious," he said thrusting into me. "I love you, too, April, with all my heart."

I lay against him, sated, listening to the beat of his heart.
He loved me.

CHAPTER 10

Three days later, Will led me up to my bedroom at The Rosebud. The renovations were over, and he was doing a final private walk through with me. I had been troubled when he got down to it right after supper in my new state of the art kitchen. I would have been perfectly happy to go back out to the barn and spend the night snuggling on the featherbed, but he was suddenly all business.

After his declaration of love three days ago, I was in a mood to indulge him, so I'd obediently fallen into step with him. As we walked though the inn, I marked items off the checklist. Having inspected the downstairs and guestrooms, we were now onto her private quarters.

"Well," he asked, teasingly arching his brow.

"Magnificent work, I must say," I said with a smile, meaning every word. The hardwood floors glowed, the woodwork was crisp, and my kitchen was a joy to work in.

"Excellent," he said, adding, "I aim to keep my clients satisfied."

Brushing against him, I teased, "I'm satisfied, cowboy."

Reaching for the doorknob for her bedroom, he turned to look at me. "Now, this room I worked on all by myself. It's my gift to you."

Touched, I stood beside him, waiting impatiently for him to open the door. "So, show me."

"Close your eyes first," he insisted.

Smiling, I complied, sweeping them shut. "Fine, they're closed. Dazzle me, cowboy."

I heard the door open and moved a few paces forward as he tugged me inside. When he let go of my hand, I stopped and waited.

"Okay, now open your eyes, precious."

Opening my eyes, I blinked in disbelief. The room glowed with the light of a hundred candles. Rose petals covered the hardwood floor, oriental carpet, and the new four-poster bed.

Will must have cleaned out every florist shop in town to get this many rose petals. The heady bouquet hung in the air, making me dizzy, or maybe it was the man by my side. He'd turned this room into a secret, seductive nook for the two of us.

I turned to look at him, moved. "It's beautiful, Billy."

Embarrassed, I flushed. I always lapsed back to calling him Billy when I was flustered.

He just smiled back at me indulgently.

Pulling a jeweler's case out of his pocket, he dropped down on one knee.

Speechless, I watched him, my eyes widening. Did he mean to...

When he flipped it open to reveal a beautiful solitaire engagement ring, I forgot to breathe for a moment.

Reaching for my trembling hand, he declared, "April, you are my love, my life. Please say you'll marry me, precious."

Smiling with tears in my eyes, I could only nod. Sniffing back tears, I managed to blurt out, "Yes, I'll marry you. I love you with all my heart."

Slipping the ring on my finger, he tugged me down into his waiting arms and we kissed, rolling in the rose petals.

MONICA'S MANHUNT

Julie Castle

CHAPTER 1

Matt Shepard walked up to Spice with all the grim determination of a man approaching a firing squad. Squiring Monica Landers out for dinner and conversation would be boring as hell, but it was for the best. A little boredom would take the edge off his frustration. It'd been three months since he'd gotten laid. A record for him. To say he was tense was an understatement.

Working overtime to finish contracts and free Will up for his honeymoon had put a severe crimp in his social life. It was the least he could do as his brother's best man. Now, he and Monica, April's maid of honor, had the bachelor party and bridal shower to plan. As far as he was concerned, a keg of beer and a stripper in Red's back room would suffice for the guys, but he had a feeling the mystery woman he was taking on this duty date wouldn't agree. It still didn't make sense to him that the wallflower he'd barely noticed in high school would own Spice, a shop that specialized in marital aids and slinky lingerie.

Sunset glittered off the plate glass window, showing off the lacy lingerie on display. Personally, he preferred bare skin to satin and lace. Less to get in the way of his goal. It was the way he preferred his hook-ups these days—short and hot, with no strings attached. He wasn't walking into that minefield again.

An overhead bell tinkled as he opened the door. He forced himself to go inside. He'd never set foot in the place before, mainly because his kid sister, Courtney, worked here as a designer, much to his displeasure. Ms. Landers would insist on being picked up here, he only hoped she wouldn't prove as obstinate when planning the pre-wedding festivities. At least her shop was empty at closing time. In fact, he didn't see his date anywhere. Not that he expected to recognize her. She was three years older than him, and they'd never moved in the same social circles. He'd been into sports, fast cars, and girls. To the best of his recollection, she'd been into the library and home economics.

He approached the counter, his sex-starved gaze lingering as it passed over the delights—lingerie, massage oils, and a wide array of sex toys. His eyes widened while his manhood stirred in reaction. The stimulation was enough to jump-start him into a hard-on.

The swing on display in the corner caught his eye. It was just like the one in April's barn, a place he'd steered clear of. He quickly looked away. Thinking about his brother's possible love life wasn't something he'd do. Ignoring the toys and lubes, Matt's gaze strayed to the lingerie hanging on a rack nearby instead. Soft, shimmering in a rainbow of colors, tempting him to reach out and touch to see if they were as soft as they looked, it almost made him change his mind about preferring his lovers nude.

A quick footfall made Matt spin around in time to see a woman rush out of the back room carrying a big box. This had to be his date. What had April called her...Modest Monica?

Matt stood there, transfixed by her intensity as she moved at breakneck speed in stiletto heels. She was beautiful, with tip tilted green eyes. Honest to Pete, they were as green as the clovers growing wild in his paddock. He stared at her, entranced, having never seen anything quite like their color before. Her mouth was generous and sensual, ripe for kissing. Her chestnut brown hair was swept up in a twist. It left her swanlike neck bare, tempting him to lean in and taste her sexy nape.

Her perfume, something light and floral, tantalized him, and he indulged in a deep whiff. She was dressed in a formfitting red dress with a row of small pearl buttons down the front. It enhanced her full curves, and it sent a jolt directly to his groin. He'd been celibate too damned long. His gaze drifted down her long bare legs to her feet arched in impossibly high heels.

"Whoa," Monica said with a gasp, spotting the quiet man standing in her shop at the last second before she collided with him, almost choking on the strawberry hard candy she was sucking on. Coughing, all she could do was stare at him as her heart skipped a beat.

Wow! Perfect. He was positively the yummiest man she'd ever set eyes on, and he was staring at her with the steamiest look in his baby blue eyes. Tall, with dirty blond hair, and a dirtier smile on his handsomer than sin face, he brought out all her repressed desires.

Dressed in a butter-soft leather jacket and faded jeans, he looked like he'd just stepped off the pages of one of her favorite erotic romances. *The Sundance Kid* in the flesh. This had to be Will's kid brother Matt. Now she understood why April had urged her to add him to her manhunt list. Too bad, he was too wild to be manhunt material. She stumbled, wobbling as her heels sunk into the carpeting, and the box she was carrying toppled.

Sundance grabbed the box with one of his big hands and her bare arm with the other. She let out a startled gasp at the heat of that seemingly innocent contact. His hands were big, work-roughened, and warm. His fingertips sensually rubbing her arm, he looked deep into her eyes, making her shiver. It was as if he could read her errant thoughts, her desires.

"Yummy," she murmured.

"What?"

"You," she said, studying him.

He broke into a startled grin that turned him from yummy to devastating. "Thanks. I think you're pretty scrumptious, too. Care to take a nibble?" he asked leaning forward to kiss her.

She watched his irises contract as he came closer, blotting everything else out, and was mesmerized. Her breath caught in her throat as his hot mouth slanted over hers, and her body turned to pudding. Her knees actually wobbled, and she fell against him, their bodies colliding, setting off sparks inside her.

He was brawny, easily supporting her weight as his hungry mouth devoured hers. She gasped, her nipples tingling, jutting toward him through the sheer fabric of her satin bra and rayon dress. She couldn't stop her tongue from snaking out to taste his lower lip, making him groan in response, but confirming her conclusion that he was definitely edible before pulling away.

He let her go with a primal growl.

She stepped back, her face flaming, and tried not to fall under his macho spell, but found it an impossible task. She couldn't deny he set her sex-starved hormones humming. Her gaze focused on Sweet Surrender, the couples' role-play bondage kit hanging on the shelf behind him. Hell yeah, he could handcuff her to the bedposts any time as he had his way with her. Rejecting her errant thoughts, she jerked away, the box slipped through his fingers, and landed on the floor. Dozens of items spilled out, littering the carpet at their feet.

"My bunnies," she wailed as he tromped on one with in his size 13 cowboy boots. "Please don't step on them."

Her bunnies?

Matt looked down at the vibrators strewn across the floor and felt his cock throb while his mouth watered. He could still taste her. Like strawberries. He wasn't sure what foolishness had made him claim her mouth, but he wasn't sorry he'd done it.

In a rainbow of different colors, the vibrators bore the label The Jack Rabbit. He gazed at the red one lying across the toe of his cowboy boot and actually felt his heart race. Good gravy.

Suddenly, his date seemed like heaven in three-inch red high heels. He looked back at her, intrigued, and couldn't help gazing at the generous swell of her breasts for a long beat before focusing on her laughing eyes. She met his gaze with a knowing glint. He knew he was ogling her tits, but it didn't stop his hungry gaze from devouring every luscious inch of her body. When she'd pressed against him, he'd felt her stiff nipples, and now he couldn't help focusing on them, beaded against her red dress. They were two ripe berries waiting for his attention, probably tasted like strawberries, and he was happy to oblige.

"Well, I guess we broke the ice and settled the yummy question once and for all, didn't we Matthew?"

Her melodious voice only made him harder as he looked back at her. "That's Matt, darlin'. And what's the decision?" He watched her nibble her lower lip, and felt his pulse race. He had a better use for those luscious lips. Her sultry gaze swept over him focusing for a long minute on his crotch. Oh yeah, she was checking him out. It made his cock strain against his zipper to get at her.

He wanted her with an intensity that surprised him, and it went way beyond craving a piece of ass. It was weird, but he felt an instant connection.

"I'll tell you later. It's a good thing for you it's restocking night, or you'd have missed me. Now, if you can keep those cowboy boots off the merchandise, I'll get on with it." She crouched to pick up her vibrators.

"Huh?" Her teasing, semi-scolding tone caught him off guard. He crouched to help her, wincing as his tight jeans compressed his burgeoning erection. He helped her scoop them up, then stood and picked up the box, despite her protest. He wasn't going to let her break her neck again. "Where do you want them?"

"I need to hang them on the wall display before I count down the till."

"I'll do it while you finish up," he insisted, almost surprised at himself. Any excuse to stay near her and extend the sensual buzz, he was suddenly a sucker for erotic punishment. He couldn't help it. He found her irresistible. She wasn't a girl, but a grown woman, who knew her own mind, and a definite challenge.

"Okay," she said after a moment. "I'll ring out, then go get my bag so we can slip out the back."

He hung the vibrators on the display racks, ultra aware of her movements, and the hot glances she kept shooting his way as she closed out the register.

Their gazes met, and she actually blushed.

He groaned under his breath as she scurried off into the backroom.

She didn't have to act like she was afraid he was going to jump her bones. Maybe he'd misread her interest. The thought made him depressed.

He went back to work, restocking her vibrators. He sure as hell had never handled one before. They were veined and semi-lifelike, if one didn't count the day-glow color, and they had another small protuberance. Intrigued, he found himself reading the package spiel—The Jack Rabbit Elite features a triple-tongued clitoral tickler and a realistic six-inch shaft for her pleasure.

He let out a groan, and stopped reading before he did himself permanent damage. Some guys might find it intimidating. He didn't. He couldn't stop himself from thinking about all the sexual possibilities it presented if he used it on her. Hell, this whole store gave him ideas. Maybe she was right to keep her distance. He'd been celibate too long. What was taking her so long?

Monica stood in the back room, eyes closed, breathing hard, her whole body trembling in reaction. He was handling her bunnies like he was amused by them, not threatened, as most men would be. Something about a woman's sex toy wielded by a confident male made her weak in the knees.

Matt Shepard was positively the hottest man she'd ever set eyes on, much less kissed. It was enough to make her drool.

More than his good looks attracted her. There was a sensual essence to the man. It told her he knew how a woman craved to be touched. Heck-fire, she wouldn't even need her vibrator with him around. Her nipples were still tingling points, her pussy growing dewy with need.

She'd been very selective since her divorce, maybe too selective if a hunk's kiss had her trembling on the brink of orgasm, but being badly burned could do that to a woman's confidence. April's upcoming nuptials had been like a slap to the side to the head, vividly reminding Monica that her biological clock was ticking. And while she rejoiced in April's happiness, she couldn't help being a wee bit envious.

It was high time she found a reliable mate, so she'd gone about it in her usual methodical way. She'd decided to go on a manhunt. Luckily, the other bridesmaids were in the same boat, so they'd joined forces.

Together, they'd compiled lists of prospective mates with April acting as an advisor. With her success in actually bagging Will, she was a fount of informative manhunt tips. Only problem was, April had been dead wrong about Matt. Yummy, yes, manhunt material, no. He was a well-known player. Hadn't he just stolen a kiss without permission? The fact she'd gleefully kissed him back, she chose to ignore. It was a good thing she'd resisted April's urging to put Matt Shepard on her list. Her raging hormones would probably win out over her head if he were on it. He'd do her like a stud, but leave her empty and wanting more. She couldn't risk it.

Letting out a cleansing breath, she succeeded in stamping down the remnants of her lingering physical reaction. With her pulse slowing to near normal, she picked up her tote bag, and then went back out to face Matt.

He'd finished hanging up the vibrators and had moved on to browse through one of her favorite lingerie displays. He was examining an emerald green silk teddy she'd personally designed. She watched him stroke it, his big workman's hands gently running over the silk, and bit back a sigh as she imagined him stroking her inside the slinky garment.

Something about him brought out all her forbidden desires. She couldn't help focusing on the prominent bulge in his jeans. Oh yeah, he had what it took to satisfy a woman. No bunnies needed with him around. He'd dressed with care in what looked like new jeans, boots, and a western shirt, and it touched her that he'd gone to so much trouble.

"Ready?" she asked.

He turned to look at her and his smile widened. "Always."

There were two ways to take that, and she studiously went for the clean one. Given half a chance, she'd tumble into his arms like a ripe plum, but it wasn't going to happen. He didn't fit the bill.

Heading for the back door, she couldn't help walking faster as he fell into step behind her. Her knees shook as his scent wrapped around her, something musky, and all man.

Dizzy with sensory overload, her knees quivered and her high heels wobbled on the carpeting.

Matt reached out to steady her, wrapping one of his big hands around her bare arm. She gasped, the tantalizing contact making her burn, her body overheating again. Ripe for the picking, she found him hard to resist, but she couldn't pick him if she wanted to find Mr. Right. She wanted it all this time—a husband, kids, stability—and the hunk clinging to her arm didn't add up to husband material.

"Thanks," she said pulling away.

"My pleasure, darlin'."

She loved the way he called her *darlin'*. The way his honeyed voice washed over her body, making her face flush, as she turned to lock the shop's back door behind them.

"This way to my truck," he said, steering her toward a black pickup.

She let him seat her, thinking about pulling out and taking her Volvo instead. But how would that look? Something told her he'd take it as a challenge. It'd probably be like waving a red cape before a charging bull. She smiled at the image because it fit him, and smoothed her dress out on her legs, tugging it down to cover her bared thighs.

Clicking her seatbelt closed, she inched toward the door. He got in and slanted a sly grin at her, like he knew what she was feeling. He probably did. Something told her he could read women very well.

"I don't bite."

"I don't believe that for a minute," she shot back at him with a wry smile as the temperature around her shot up. She had a feeling it had more to do with Matt than the balmy evening air. "I believe you said you made reservations at Finnegan's Supper Club."

"Right, darlin', unless you'd rather just chuck it all and go to Red's."

The cheerfully voiced suggestion told her all she needed to know. He might be fun to toy with, but he was too wild to be husband material. "No, thanks." She took her duty as April's maid of honor seriously, even if he didn't value his role as best man as much.

"Right you are. We've got Cupid's work to do, don't we?" He gunned the engine. "Hold tight, and we'll be there in two shakes."

"Cupid's work?" she parroted, startled by the sensitive phrase coming out of his made-to-kiss mouth. Maybe he'd gotten it off a Hallmark card. She slanted an assessing gaze his way. The final bright rays of the setting sun highlighted his handsome face, turned his hair to honey and frosted the plains of his powerfully toned body with gold. He had the kind of silhouette made for a woman's delight. She watched them thrust the keys into the ignition as if it was the most fascinating thing in the world and, at the moment, it was. She couldn't help being powerfully sexually aware of him.

He was looking her over just as curiously. The very air seemed filled with passionate promise, one she shouldn't keep if she was serious about finding Mr. Right instead of Mr. Right Now. Still, he was alluring, his broad shoulders seemed to almost brush hers in the pickup's cab. She watched his long thick fingers on the steering wheel and couldn't keep from thinking about them caressing her, slipping inside her as he kissed her until she couldn't think straight. Her lips tingled as she focused on his.

He grinned at her. "I'm not all beer and pool, darlin'. I want to make sure that this one's a keeper."

"April is." She instantly shot to her friend's defense, but his tone hadn't been accusatory, just cautionary. It made her wonder why. What made him so gun-shy about women?

"Calm down, I didn't mean it that way. I don't doubt it for a minute that they're made for each other. Kind of nice, those two finding each other."

"Magical," she said with a nod. At least they agreed on one point. Maybe they would mesh, maybe he should be on her manhunt list.

"Not that I think every guy should be married," he said under his breath.

She let out a sigh, mentally scratching his name off the list. "It made me think," she said, pretending she hadn't heard him.

"About what?"

"Getting married," she said, and instantly felt him tense beside her. That cooled his ardor, darn it. Maybe it was for the best.

"You're engaged?" His gaze shot to her bare left hand. "You aren't wearing a ring."

She glanced at her left hand. That was true. The white line from her wedding band had faded away two years ago. "No. I'm not engaged."

"Engaged to be engaged then?" he asked in a curious tone.

"No. I don't even have a lover." She felt his interest pick up when she said the L word, and decided to give him a cold shower and cool it permanently for her own good. "I'm on a manhunt to find a husband."

She was both relieved and heartsick when he didn't say anything in response. It was for the best, so why did she still feel like seeing him naked?

CHAPTER 2

Matt was still trying to come up with a response when he escorted Monica into the supper club. She was on a manhunt to find a husband! He felt like a marked man for the steamy things he'd fantasized about doing with her. Her taste, and the feel of her soft lips pressed against his, still haunted him. He wanted to taste her all over despite her warning that she was marriage minded.

Taking her arm as he ushered her inside, he felt her tremble in response to his touch, and it only made him hotter, hornier. At least he had the pleasure of knowing she was just as attuned to him.

She was pissed at him because of his automatic negative reaction to the subject of marriage, he could tell, and she was turned on by their sexual chemistry at the same time. He knew the telltale symbols of a woman's arousal, her sneak peeks at him, her quick breaths, the way she licked her luscious lips and damned near ate him up with her hungry eyes. He reciprocated, but he was going to come out of this limping if he didn't find some way to turn off his body's natural reaction to her. Going around with a permanent hard-on wasn't healthy for a man of his age. What the hell was a dyed in the wool bachelor like him supposed to say to the news that she was husband-hunting?

When he saw Carrie Summers working at the restaurant's hostess station, he wanted to turn around and steer Monica in the other direction. Blonde, petite, and twenty-two, she'd been his last date, kind of. He'd been so bored after an hour, he took her home early, saying he was sick.

"Reservations for Shepard," he said, hoping she wouldn't remember him.

Her eyes narrowed with irritation as she looked him over, and he knew his luck had run out.

"Reservations, you say?" She arched one plucked brow.

"Yes," he murmured, relieved. At least she wasn't giving him a hard time. Maybe he'd come out of this unscathed.

Carrie ignored him and, instead, gave Monica a curious once over.

"Fancy you actually called for reservations, Shepard. I thought your phone didn't work. After all, you never called me back like you said you would."

Crap. Matt heard Monica chuckle at his side and stiffened. She was definitely enjoying his discomfort. Famous last words he couldn't live down, *I'll call you sometime, Carrie.* He'd said it to soothe her ruffled pride after he'd dropped her at her door without a goodnight kiss, not that he could tell her that now. Who'd have thought that this woman couldn't read between the lines. Monica definitely would have gotten the message, but she was worlds apart from Carrie.

Still, standing there on the spot, he scrambled for a way out. "About that, after our fizzled date I figured—"

"Yeah, it did end badly." She glanced down at his crotch and shrugged. "Thanks for reminding me."

He wanted to sink into the ground. Now Monica, no doubt, thought he couldn't get it up. Nothing could be further from the truth. He'd been just dog-tired that night, and sick of one-night stands.

"Follow me," Carrie said, picking up menus and leading them to their table.

With all other options fading, Matt bit back his comeback that he could so get it up, and followed. What did it matter? Monica wasn't on the menu for the evening, so correcting the wrong impression didn't matter.

Glancing around the supper club, he noticed several pairs of curious eyes on them, especially from three of the guys at the bar. Then he realized they weren't really focused on him, they were ogling his date. If he'd reconciled himself to the fact that Monica couldn't be his, why did the fact that none of the single guys at the bar could take their eyes off her bother him? It was a question he didn't want to answer, so he decided to concentrate on the competition instead.

Slowing, he scowled back at them. The worst offenders looked away. When he pulled Monica's chair out to seat her, he could tell she was surprised at his attempt at gallantry, but she slipped into her seat, giving him an assessing look.

His hands brushed against her sides as he slid her chair ahead. The sensation of warm silk, and even warmer woman, made him groan under his breath. She was so enticing. She made him swell with need. He felt her hot gaze on him as he walked around the table and sat down. He was most definitely still on the make, he couldn't help it, and it was as natural as breathing to him.

He watched her pick up her menu, but didn't touch his. Just looking at her made him hungry, and he was suddenly overwhelmed with the need to correct things.

"I don't have a problem with..."

"Don't worry, it happens to most guys. You were probably just tired."

His mouth snapped shut as she rushed in to save his supposedly wounded male pride. After taking a deep cleansing breath, like the Yoga tape April had lent him taught him to do, he pinned Monica with a steady look. Her violet eyes were soft with sympathy, and it made him frustrated.

"Listen, lady, I've never had any complaints in bed."

"Um, right." Her doubtful gaze drifted back to Carrie, who stood at the hostess station staring at them.

He turned his back on Carrie making steady eye contact with Monica instead. "I just told her that to get rid of her."

"I'm sure you did."

He knew pity when he heard it, and it made him crazy. How in the hell could he prove he could still get it up? He wracked his brain for a clean way that wouldn't embarrass her. Gazing at her soft lips, he remembered the kiss. He'd shot from stiff to rampant as she'd pressed against him.

"Need I remind you of my yummy factor?" he asked, and watched her telltale reaction. Her cheeks turned a fetching rose as she blushed.

"Right, funny me, forgetting a little thing like that."

"Little," he groused, and then saw the teasing twinkle in her eyes. "Tell me about your manhunt, darlin'."

"Why?"

"Curiosity." He watched her nibble her bottom lip and his blood heated, while his cock throbbed. "Maybe I can give you a few pointers, one player to another."

"So, that's what you think I am, a player?"

To his surprise, she almost sounded hurt. "Yeah. A babe that owns a sex-toy shop and goes after things directly. I'd call you a player."

"You'd be wrong then."

Her downcast expression startled him. "Sorry. It was meant as a compliment, I didn't mean anything bad by that. It's refreshing to meet a woman who lays all her cards on the table and doesn't try to trap a man under false pretenses."

"From your grim tone, it sounds like you've got personal experience at that one."

He felt her interest, and it made him tense. She really seemed to care about the details of his love life, but he couldn't discuss that now, hadn't been able to since he'd dragged his beaten ass back home. "My mamma always told me a gentleman never kisses and tells."

"Smart mamma," she said with a grin.

"Right." Her open smile made his tension roll away. He reached out to touch her hand. "I'm sorry. I never intended to insult you by calling you a player."

She squeezed his hand before pulling away. "Don't worry about bruising my tender feelings. I should be used to it by now. Most guys assume I'm swinging off the chandeliers, throwing wild orgies. Nothing could be further from the truth. Nice guys never ask me out, and frankly, I frequently have to fend off jerks. It's been three years since I—"

"Hush now," he cut in her admission, making him feel for her. And he thought three months without sex was a long dry spell.

She blushed. "I don't know why I blurted that out. How embarrassing."

"Don't worry about it."

"It's not that I haven't had any offers. It's just that they weren't the right kind. Maybe you're right, a player who owns a sex-toy shop, how likely am I to find a mate?"

"I don't think that," he said, meaning every word. She'd make an ideal playmate for the right guy.

He scowled at the three guys who were watching them from the bar again. Two looked away, but one just kept on staring. Ted Miller. Matt recognized the tall and chunky former high school football star. The guy was starting to turn fat, as the spare tire around his middle under his red polo shirt showed. He'd heard of the guy, and what he'd heard wasn't good. Arrogant and a card cheat, and he had a bad reputation as a sneaky bastard with the good old boys who hung out at Red's.

Suppressing an overwhelming need to go punch him out, Matt instead turned back to Monica. She was blushing again, even though her eyes were twinkling. A modest, sometimes bawdy, sex goddess, it boggled his mind, and threatened to drive him crazy. "There's an innocence about you that shines through, darlin'."

She leaned forward, looking deep into his eyes. "Where'd that come from?"

He felt like he was on top of the world as she seemed to hang on every word he said. The feeling was mutual, but a rational part of his mind said to beware. Still, he had to know what she was thinking. "Damned if I know. So, spill it, tell me about your manhunt."

Her hand clutched the tote bag she used as a purse. "You want to see it?"

"It?" He watched her open the bag and paw through the cluttered contents—lipstick, powder, strawberry shaped candies, and a tube of something. "You mean you've got it down on paper?"

"Of course." She pulled out a red leather bound planner and opened it, handing it over with a flourish. "Maybe you can give me a few suggestions. You know the men around these parts."

He looked down at the list of pro's and con's written in an elegant script and raised a brow. "Wow, nerd alert."

"Yeah, I tend to be a bit analytical," she agreed with a wry smile. "It's what makes me a good businesswoman."

Relieved she hadn't taken offense, he glanced back at the planner.

"Pro. Having love and companionship. Con. Opening myself up to pain."

"Pro. My biological clock is ticking. Con. Might not be a good mother."

He looked at her. She was watching him in anticipation, seeming to really care what he thought, her head tilted, her lips parted, a worried gleam in her eyes. He couldn't help warming himself on her playful, joyful essence for a moment before he said, "You'll be a good mom, Monica."

She smiled at him. "Thanks."

"Pro. Being sexually satisfied. Con. What if he can't perform?"

He'd already settled the performance issue, and it was true he never had any complaints. But she wasn't talking about him, she was talking about some nameless jerk who'd be her mate. His gut clenched. Did he really want to read more? He had to know what he was up against. Without comment, he turned to the next page.

"Hmm, let's take a look at the qualifications your baby's daddy will need. He's got to be gainfully employed," he read.

"I want a man with ambition." She nodded.

"He needs to make as much money as I do."

"Right, I don't want a man whose ego is threatened by my business."

"He must be settled and dependable."

"Yes."

"Hmm." He looked up at her flushed face. "Do you mean boring?"

"No. I mean I don't want a man who'll get distracted by the next pair of tits that comes along."

He gazed at her ample cleavage. "Somehow, I doubt that could happen."

"Thanks," she said with a laugh. "You're good for my ego, Junior."

Junior! He scowled at her. "What's with the Junior business? I'm only three years younger than you."

"Ah yes, but women mature much faster than men."

He didn't like where this was heading. "Which means I'm not steady and dependable."

"Right, so relax, you're not on the list."

He scowled and turned the page. He should have been happy about that, but he wasn't. He gazed at the list, there had to be twenty names on it. Damn. Some of them were actually decent guys, not that he was going to tell her that. And then his gaze strayed to number six—Ted Miller, and he tensed. She sure as hell didn't know what she was doing, to have jerk-wad Ted on the list of candidates. How could he knock him off without sounding like a jealous ass?

"Do they know they're contenders for matrimony?"

"Heavens no. They'd probably run in the other direction if they did. It's all arranged. I'm going to go on a series of casual dates and put them to the test."

"Dates?"

"Right, starting tomorrow night with number one. Who knows, maybe I'll find someone special to be my date for the wedding reception."

The waitress walked up to their table carrying a frosty drink on a tray. "For you, Monica. Compliments of the gentleman at the bar." She set the drink in front of Monica with a flourish, handed her a note, and then gave Matt a wink. "Sorry stud, he didn't send anything for you."

Matt scowled at the waitress's sassy smile. "I'm not giving you a tip."

She smiled at him. "I already got it."

Monica took a sip of the margarita, then turned to smile at the man standing at the bar who'd sent it.

"Who the sent that?" Matt grumbled, already knowing the answer.

"Number six," she said, distracted. "Ted Miller, orthodontist. He has a thriving practice in Center City."

He glared at Ted. "He drinks and cheats at cards."

"Who?"

"Miller there, lurking at the bar." Only the lowest kind of jerk tried to poach from another man while he was on a date. Miller's face was flushed as he joked with his buddies at the bar.

"And I should care that he cheats at cards, why?"

Matt took his watchful gaze off his rival to glance at Monica. "A man who cheats at cards can't be trusted."

She nodded, seemed to digest that for a moment, but he could feel her doubt. He had to use more persuasive tactics.

"Now, about these other jokers—"

"If you'll excuse me, I think I'll go freshen up." She quickly got to her feet, picked up her tote bag, and slipped her planner into it.

He watched her retreat to the ladies' room, and came to a decision. She didn't know what she was doing, so he had to save her from the list.

Monica stood in the bathroom, running cold water on her wrists to cool down. She'd known she had to get away when Matt had adopted that scolding tone and started demolishing her list. Getting lost in Matt's sexy blue eyes wasn't going to get her married. She'd had a ladies' man before. She didn't want another one.

Although, to lump Matt in with a loser like her ex-husband Gary wasn't fair. Gary was verbally abusive, along with being a crook and a cheat. Through luck and a tenacious will to survive, she'd taken the small gift shop her parents had left her and turned it into Spice during the turmoil of her divorce. Without it, she might have drowned in the sea of his debts. Instead, she'd been able to make restitution to those he'd bilked and build a life for herself. And now it was time to find someone to share it with.

Matt Shepard, while being dreamy, wasn't a marrying man. He'd been direct about it. She winced, remembering his blunt statement about marriage not being for him.

Drying her hands, she went out to meet him. Maybe she'd at least get a goodbye kiss out of the evening, another taste of magic before she settled down with boring Mr. Right.

She walked down the shadowy hall back to the dining room, when a hand grabbed her from behind. She let out a squeak of alarm as she was hauled backwards against a doughy body that reeked of alcohol and cologne. She didn't even have to look to know who it was. Matt had been right about him.

"What the hell do you think you're doing?" She scowled at Ted, leering down at her.

"What's the matter, baby?" he asked with a cool smile. "Doesn't my drink at least get me a kiss and a cuddle?"

She scowled and brought her stiletto down on his instep.

He howled with pain and let her go.

"You bitch!" he yelled, hopping on one foot, drawing back his hand to slap her. "Gary was right. You are a cold hearted tramp."

Gary! The name hit her like a chilling blast. She knew her ex had long tentacles, as proved by his threatening letters from prison, but this was totally unexpected.

While the sickening revelation she'd added a friend of Gary's to her manhunt sunk in, she bobbed away, adopting a fighting stance. She hadn't studied self-defense for nothing. Number six was about to get his ass kicked.

Ted froze instead of striking her, and looked at a spot beyond her.

She let out a sigh of relief. Matt! Even as she thought it, she knew it was him. She turned to find him standing quietly behind her.

His protective gaze flicked over her for a millisecond. "You okay, darlin'?"

She nodded. "I am now. Thanks for the backup."

"My pleasure." His gaze slammed back to Ted.

Miller sneered at Matt for a moment before dropping his gaze and backing off. "Slut like her ain't worth the trouble, buddy."

Matt growled and tried to step around her.

"No." She grabbed his hand to stop him. Although the name wasn't pleasant, she was used to it. She'd been called worse, and she didn't want Matt to get in trouble.

She let out the breath she'd been holding as Matt obeyed and cradled her in his arms instead. She sagged against him as he rubbed her tight shoulders.

"I was worried about you," Matt murmured into her ear.

She trembled against him, secure in his strength. "I guess you were right about him."

"Then, you'll—"

"Cross him off the list," she completed with an emphatic nod. She smiled as he wrapped his arms tighter around her.

A man who could intimidate an aggressor without saying a word, now that was impressive.

"Let's get out of here, babe."

She took a calming breath, reveling in his strength surrounding her, drawing in his essence, and felt her serenity restored. "I'm with you, babe."

"Babe?" he asked, raising a brow.

"I'm just trying it out. I should come up with some cutesy name for you if I'm *darlin'* and *babe*. How about *Mr. Amazing*?"

"Sounds like I should be wearing a cape and tights." He chuckled.

"You're not the tights type," she said as they headed out the door. "How about *snuggle bunny*, then?"

"Good gravy," he muttered, opening her pickup truck door and helping her in.

She laughed out loud at his outraged glower. "How about *sweetie pie*," she said as he started the truck and pulled away.

His grin told her he didn't mind that.

"Okay, sweetie pie it is." Looking at him in the moon's glow, she whispered, "And sometimes, Sundance."

That's how she'd think of him when she fantasized about him—and she *would* fantasize about him. No man had ever come to her rescue before, and she couldn't quite wrap her mind around it. He was almost too good to be true, and she had him at least for tonight.

When he dropped her off, she was going to give him a goodnight kiss that would knock his socks off.

CHAPTER 3

Monica couldn't take her eyes off Matt as he drove them along the lake. Her senses were simmering. The soft feel of his lips on hers lingered. She wanted to kiss him again, harder, deeper. He was Mr. Wrong, but tonight, he was Mr. Amazing. His chiseled profile in the moonlight tempted her to reach out and touch it. Run her fingers down his cheek, trace his sensual mouth, make him pull over and kiss her until she couldn't think straight.

He slanted a quick sidelong glance at her. "Pencil me in."

"What?" She watched his lips move, but could hardly believe the words were coming out of his hunky mouth. He couldn't really want on the manhunt list.

"You heard me," he said, his focus snapping back to the road ahead.

His determined tone made her shiver with delight, even though she knew it was a pipe dream. "Calm down, Matt, it's just your raging testosterone talking. Almost getting in a fight will do that to a man."

"Know that firsthand, do ya?" he asked dryly.

Unfortunately, she did, not that she was going to tell him that. Her ex's favorite pastime was picking fights with any guy he even thought was looking her way. It was one of his favorite tactics for keeping her off balance so she wouldn't notice he was robbing her blind, not to mention cheating on her. She'd been young and foolish enough to be manipulated. Now, she was a grown woman who knew her own mind. How could she boil that down into one simple sentence?

She simply shrugged.

"Darlin', I was defending your honor, not looking for a fight. Anyhow, Ted Miller ran like a scared rabbit."

"I noticed." It was true, he'd intimidated Ted without throwing a punch. Still, she knew in the morning he'd change his mind about being on the manhunt list. Maybe giving him a knock down, curl his toes, goodnight kiss wasn't such a good idea. "Thanks for the offer, it's sweet of you, but my advice is to go home and take a cold shower. As for me, when I use my bunny, I'll think of you, if that helps."

His hands tightened on the truck's steering wheel. "Thanks for the case of blue balls, lady. Oh yeah, that just does it for me."

She winced in sympathy. She understood frustrated desire better than most. It wasn't easy running Spice and not having anyone to try her sexy wares with. A nice quiet husband would solve that problem.

"When you find some little nymph to pleasure you, you can think of me. Maybe ask Carrie out again. She's about your age." Even as she said it, the image of him with another woman made her sick at heart.

"For your information, Carrie is a twenty-two-year-old twit," he said dryly, turning down a country lane. "I'm a grown man, in case you hadn't noticed."

She'd definitely noticed. She held her breath as she became aware of the lane they were traveling, and guessed exactly where they were going—lover's lane. She hadn't been out here since she'd watched the submarine races in high school. It tickled her. She had to give him an A for action.

She couldn't help inching closer as she murmured, "I noticed, sweetie pie."

He said something soft and sweet under his breath.

"That does it," he said, pulling off into a secluded overlook. The city lights twinkled below. "How about I give you a demonstration of my eagerness? A free sample to prove I can perform, so you'll put me on the list."

She smiled despite her better judgment as she gazed at his intent expression in the moonlight. She was glad they had the parking spot all to themselves.

"You've got to be kidding. I know you really don't want to be on the list."

"Does this seem like a joke?" He leaned forward and kissed her, his mouth slanting hungrily across hers.

She went into his arms with a sigh of surrender, aching to kiss him. She'd needed to taste him again. His mouth molded hers, and it was even better than she remembered. She sighed, her lips parting under his, and put her arms around him.

Her seatbelt unsnapped as he unfastened it and pulled her to him. It thrilled her to hear him growl deep in his throat as he deepened the kiss. She burned, her whole body heating. Her nipples stiffened, rubbing against her satin bra, tingling, her pussy wet. More than wet—aching, needy. She whimpered, pressing tight to him.

"That's it, babe, burn for me." He cupped one of her breasts with his big hand and squeezed, pressing firmly against her nipple.

She gasped at the pleasure that simple but profound contact brought. He had magic hands. When he started unbuttoning the front of her dress, she let him, craving his touch, no matter what. Opening the top of her dress, his hot gaze lingered on her breasts, cupped in the red satin bra she wore, and she trembled. Never had she felt sexier, more desirable. Always well-endowed, they now seemed swollen with need, her nipples tingling.

"Darlin', you're so beautiful."

"Thank you," she murmured, embarrassed. Nobody had ever called her beautiful in that reverential tone before, certainly not her ex.

He bent to take her nipple in his mouth, lapping at it through her bra. It was the most erotic thing she'd ever experienced. She whimpered, turning into a puddle of desire against him, and arched toward that teasing tongue. It'd been so long since she'd been touched. Her hands found their way inside his shirt, running along his body. Firm and resilient, it was like touching hot satin. He arched into her touch like a big cat.

He pulled her tighter to him, his hand slipping under her dress to cup her mound. "You're so hot, babe."

She pulsed in his hot hand against her needy sex, and felt like she'd died and gone to heaven. It felt so good to be held like this, his palm applying gentle pressure that made her pant.

"You have no idea," she gasped, nibbling his ear, her tongue flicking at it. She hissed with pleasure when he stroked her through her panties, his finger tracing her pussy's cleft teasingly. "Oh please," she whimpered as he drew a slow circle around her swollen clit.

"Don't worry." He growled, simultaneously slipping his hand inside her panties while he captured her nipple in his mouth.

She cried out with ecstasy, shudders of pleasure rocking her. His thick fingers filled her pussy, he found her clit with his thumb, and she came. Clinging to him, she shuddered, crying out his name as she convulsed around those teasing digits.

"That's it, darlin', come for me," he growled, tweaking her clit again.

And she did, exploding again, as he milked another orgasm out of her.

He kissed her as she slowly drifted back to earth. She reached for his zipper. Time to take things in hand. She opened his jeans to find he wasn't wearing underwear. Amused and a bit startled to see him going commando, she smiled. His cock sprang out—hot, hard, and huge in her hand, and he let out a groan.

She could only stare at it for a moment, impressed. He put her rabbits to shame. She stroked him teasingly from his red tip, moist with a drop of pre-cum, down his long veined shaft, to cup his turgid balls. He'd mentioned blue balls, but they didn't look blue to her. She looked at him, about to ask about it, and thought better of it. Some things about male anatomy, a woman just didn't need to know.

He groaned, thrusting into her hands. It was then she remembered the free sample of Good Head Gel in her tote bag. She was going to use it to lube her screen door, but why not use it for its real purpose? It was a chance to put her merchandise to the test.

She pulled the small tube out of her bag.

He gave her a questioning look. "What is that?"

"Just sit back and enjoy it, Sundance."

She opened the tube, swirling gel on his rampant cock, and he hissed in pleasure. She knew it went on cool. The sweet aroma of strawberries filled the cab of his truck. She bent to lick him, and he let out a groan. Flicking her tongue around the head of his cock, she tasted strawberries and him. With a sigh of surrender, she took him into her mouth. It made her bold and crazy to pleasure him this way. She'd never really done this before, but he didn't have to know that. He grew hot and harder in her mouth as she bobbed up and down, her pussy throbbed along with her strokes.

"Darlin', enough, or I won't be able to control myself." He gently pulled her up and kissed her.

She kissed him back in rapture, lost in the feeling of his tongue thrusting into her mouth. Now she knew what she'd been denying herself. All thought went away as he cupped her breasts, teasing the nipples into tingling points. Then, one of his hands drifted down to find the heat between her legs again. She trembled as his finger traced her cleft behind her panties and unerringly found her swollen clit. He bent to kiss her. She moaned, her eyes closed.

A blare from a car horn cut through her haze of passion, and she stiffened.

Matt let out a growl and tucked her back into the shadows. She turned to see two carloads of teens now parked next to them. She quickly pulled closed her dress, shrinking away from Matt. Good grief, they'd almost been caught in the act.

"Lord, give me strength," Matt hissed as he zipped his pants up.

She winced in sympathy, knowing it wasn't easy to tuck that monster away, and he had to be hurting. "Sorry, Sundance."

"Not half as sorry as I am, darlin'," he said, starting the truck and driving away.

Was he sorry he didn't get laid, or was he regretting his insistence about being added to her manhunt?

Matt's arousal level was banked, but still high as he drove back to town with Monica at his side. He wasn't quite sure what had happened to him, but in one short night, she'd managed to wrap herself around his heart. A glance to the side showed her hands trembling as she fastened the last button on her dress, and he was lost in fantasy.

The mingled scents of her perfume and strawberries tempted him to pull off into the bushes and finish what they'd started. He'd never eat a strawberry again without thinking about making love to her. Knowing it would probably shock her if he stopped, he kept on driving, replaying in his mind the moment her sweet lips had closed around his cock. He stifled a groan as his hard-on jump-started back into rampant. She was worth the pain. Just imagining the image of her in his bed, her hair spread out on his pillow, her lips parted in ecstasy as he took her, made him crazy.

"Drive back to Spice, okay?" she said.

"Okay." Hell yeah, that was fine with him. There were a few goodies there he'd like to use on her. He'd rub the cinnamon massage oil all over her and take his time licking it off.

The windows of her shop were dark as he approached the building.

"Around the back, please."

His arousal simmered as he pulled into the parking lot behind Spice, turned off the key, and turned to look at her in the moonlight. God, she was beautiful. He reached out to cup her soft cheek, and she leaned into his caress, her eyes shining.

"You don't..."

He bent to kiss her, cutting off her words, and she melted in his arms, going all fluid on him. He groaned as she pressed against him, his body throbbing in response, and pulled away before he made love to her right there. He had to make it inside so they'd have privacy and he could pleasure her properly.

Jerking his driver's side door open, he got out and sprinted around to open hers. She was sitting there motionless, watching him, a dazed look in her eyes.

He gently tugged her to him, stepping between her legs as she turned to get out.

"Come here, darlin'." He leaned in to kiss her, his lips brushing gently over her soft tremulous ones.

God, she tasted good. Edging closer, her dress rode up so that her bare legs were straddling him. On fire, he ran his hand up the inside of her thigh.

The sound of a throat being cleared made him freeze, his hand inches from her pussy, his lips still locked with hers. Monica stiffened for a moment before pulling away.

"I've got guests waiting for me."

He rested his forehead to hers, his thudding heartbeat slowing, as he heard female voices behind him. One of them he recognized as his sister's.

"Where?"

"My house is behind the parking lot."

"Who's here?"

"April and the bridesmaids."

He turned to see several women clustered around the front porch of the small bungalow beyond Spice's driveway. April and Courtney he recognized, and Toni, a local deputy sheriff still in uniform. Two others were strangers to him. They all sat around a wicker patio set where refreshments were set up.

"Hey, you two, break it up." Courtney said with a smile.

Matt reluctantly disengaged from Monica, scowling at his kid sister, who wasn't cowed in the least. The other females all eyed him with various stages of amusement and suspicion.

Damn. He growled, which made Monica chuckle ruefully.

"Sorry, Sundance."

Matt forced himself to back off, help her out of the truck.

"Later," he said with a promise as she kissed him on the cheek and turned away. It felt like the hardest thing he'd ever done as he let her go.

He watched her walk toward the party on her deck, then got in his pickup and drove away.

Monica went to face the inquisition she knew was coming as Matt drove away. She couldn't help gazing at his retreating tail-lights forlornly. She'd just lost what promised to be the best night of her life, which meant her love life sucked.

Sighing, she turned to face her friends, who were lounging on the wicker patio furniture on her front porch, sipping iced tea and munching on snacks. It was their usual Thursday night Manhunter's Club Meeting, and for once, she had something to report. Only, she didn't want to.

They'd formed the support group shortly after April's engagement because they were all at loose ends. Courtney and Amber, the youngest of the group, had recently broken up with their boyfriends. Both bubbly blondes, they'd probably have no trouble once they got back in the dating world. Emily, a buttoned-up librarian with her sandy brown hair in a bun and dowdy clothes, needed a makeover more than anything else. Toni, a petite redheaded cop just needed to be disarmed. Monica had been the most hopeless of them all. The manhunt had seemed like a good idea at the time. Now, she wasn't so sure. Ted Miller would have been a complete disaster.

Who the heck had suggested him anyway, she wondered, gazing at her would-be dating mavens. She couldn't think straight, much less walk a straight line, with her body still simmering from the hunk that'd almost made love to her. Her body still sensitized, her heart still racing, her steps faltered as she approached her wrap-around front porch. Her friends had her best interests at heart, but Matt wasn't a subject she wanted to discuss.

"Tell," Courtney insisted, pouring her a glass of iced tea from the pitcher sitting on the coffee table.

"What?"

"About the bridal shower of course," April said with a smile.

Monica's cheeks heated. "We didn't exactly get that far."

"Told ya." Courtney eyed April to the tune of several high fives.

"Want me to run a background check on him?" Toni offered.

"He's dating her, not trying to get a job." Brandi said.

Emily frowned. "If he's on the list, we need to do it."

April and Courtney looked at each other and frowned. "We know everything about him. No background check is needed, thank you."

"Yeah, but you weren't here all the time April, and then there was the two years he lived in Las Vegas, Courtney."

"What happens in Vegas..." April started with a grin.

"He only moved out there because there was a construction boom," Courtney cut in. "Besides, he's my brother, I'd know if he had a secret baby or a gambling problem or something."

"Sorry," Toni said. "You know I tend to be—"

"Paranoid," Courtney cut in with an indulgent smile.

She shrugged, not taking offense. "Proactive."

Monica smiled. "Ladies, let's keep this civilized. Let's just say he's a good man and leave it at that."

April smiled. "See, I told ya. It's a good thing he's on the list."

"Who says he's on the list?" Monica frowned as they all talked around her.

"Isn't he?"

She felt all eyes on her, and grew hot again. "By a mere technicality."

"Still counts." Courtney said.

"Well, at least we finally got her laid," Toni said.

"You did not."

CHAPTER 4

Monica punched her pillow for the fifth time and rolled over, trying to go back to sleep. Was it even possible for women to have wet dreams? Whatever hers were, they were certainly erotic.

Groaning, she squeezed shut her eyes and drifted into a half sleep. She and a shadowy figure were walking down an aisle and church bells were ringing—and ringing—and ringing.

Her eyes popped open and...the stupid doorbell. Yawning, she stumbled out of bed and stomped toward the front door just as some idiot started pounding on it. If it was a salesman, he was dead meat. She jerked open the door, prepared to give him a piece of her mind, and sputtered to a halt.

Matt stood there holding two styrofoam cups of coffee and a bag from Henderson's Bakery. He looked like a sex god. The rising sun's rays highlighted his hair and sultry smile as he looked her over.

She peered at him through blurry eyes. He had to be some kind of mirage. Maybe she was still dreaming. She pinched herself and gave a little yelp. "You're real," she gasped.

"In the flesh," he said, bending to brush a brief kiss on her lips. "And you're adorable." He smiled as he looked down at her nightshirt. "Teddy bears?"

"What can I say, I like bears." She could hardly believe he was here, commenting on her pajamas, at what time was it? The sun was just rising. "What time is it?"

"Six in the morning. I couldn't sleep."

"So, you decided I shouldn't sleep either?" she said with little heat in her complaint. She hadn't slept well, either. Fantasies of him kept getting in the way of slumber.

"A peace offering." Stepping across her threshold, he handed her a cup.

She wrapped her hand around the warm cup, finding his gaze even warmer as she stepped back to allow him admittance. He gave her sleepwear an amused once over. A ratty sleep tee, hardly the height of fashion for a lingerie designer, but sleeping alone, she'd opted for comfort. Although, the appreciative look in his eye as he swept up the length of her bared thighs told her he liked what he saw. Standing there, half-naked in front of the man she wanted all naked, it was all she could do not to wrestle him to the ground and demand that he do her.

Instead, she gripped her cup tighter. Thankfully, the coffee's tantalizing aroma brought her back to planet Earth. Crazy? Yeah, she had to admit she was bonkers about him. It was a good thing he didn't know her vulnerability.

She smiled at him. "You're forgiven, this time."

"So, coffee's the way to your heart?"

"It's the way into my house at six in the morning," She turned to walk into the kitchen.

She heard his footsteps trailing after her and shivered with delight. Sundance here in the flesh made her weak in the knees. They could do it in her bed or on her chaise lounge. Maybe her plush chair-and-a-half. Would her bedroom rafters support a sex swing? Her knees trembled as the thought zinged around her errant brain.

"Steady there, darlin'." He grasped her elbow to steady her.

She moaned as his warm hand closed over her bare arm. She couldn't help it. A brush fire had started inside her, ignited from where he'd touched her. His grip lightened, his fingers caressing her needy flesh. She pulled away, trying to refocus.

Putting her cup on the counter, she went to the fridge to get out the cream.

"Don't bother darlin'. Cream and two sugars."

She looked over her shoulder at him. He was leaning against the cupboards in her cozy kitchen, watching her like she was about to be dessert.

"You remembered how I take my coffee."

"I remember lots of things. Like this." He bent to brush a brief teasing kiss on her lips.

She was turning to pudding when he pulled away. She was left wanting more. Instead, he opened the bag and pulled out a still warm strawberry Danish. Her stomach growled.

"For my lady," he said, feeding her a bite.

She ate the pastry, the strawberry jam bursting on her tongue, while her eyes ate him.

The Good Head Gel was still in her bag from last night's sensual encounter in his pickup. Even as she thought it, he was reaching for her. She fell into his arms with a sigh of surrender. She kissed him back with all the burning passion she'd suppressed. She'd done nothing but dream about him all night, and hadn't even reached for her bunny once. A taste of the real thing had spoiled her for the imitation.

His hands stroked down her back, shaping her form, and squeezed her bottom. She gasped into his mouth, all but catching fire.

"Oh please," she whispered when he pulled away.

"I will, darlin'." He scooped her up in his arms and carried her to the dinette, collapsing onto a chair as she kissed him.

She wound up astride him, her bare pussy pressed against his soft washed jeans. Her swollen clit bumped up against his bulging crotch, her budding nipples tingling as they rubbed against his chest. She whimpered, unable to stop herself from rolling her hips to increase the exquisite pressure. She hissed at the waves of pleasure building in her, zinging from her sensitized clit, and gazed deep into his eyes.

He was watching her, enjoying her enjoying him. It undid her last bit of restraint.

"What are you doing to me, Sundance?" she murmured, on fire for his touch.

"Proving my worth," he said, leaning forward to nibble her nape as his arms wrapped around her.

She trembled, sagging against him, her hands clutching his shoulders because he made her feel dizzy with desire. He was growing bigger, harder against her sensitive pussy, making her tremble.

"Oh honey, you don't have to. I know the genuine article when I feel it." She rolled her hips again, gasping at the pure pleasure, and his throbbing hard-on. She watched his eyes darken in response.

He smiled, his hands slipping down to grip her bare bottom, holding her still against him. "So, did you fantasize about me, too?"

"Yes," she blurted, burned by the fire in his eyes.

So, he'd ached for her, as well. It was a balm for her raging hormones. He was obviously just barely keeping it under control. His cock growing stiffer against her, beads of sweat breaking out on his brow. She leaned forward to lap at the steady pulse in his throat, tasting his salty skin.

Hearing him groan, she murmured her confession against him. "I never even used my bunny once. I think you've spoiled it for me, Sundance."

His sexy chuckle drove her crazy on two points—it made her fantasize about what else she could do to make him make that sound again, and it pissed her off at the same time.

"It's not funny," she grumbled, nipping at his earlobe. "This is my livelihood."

He laughed. "Don't fear, darlin'. I think we can think of ways to spice up the bunny experience."

She smiled at him and snuggled closer, his erection rubbing against her sensitive mound, and she sizzled in response. "You are too good to be true, cowboy."

"Babe, the feeling's mutual." He tugged her shirt over her head, effortlessly stripping it off.

She sat there, nude, straddling him, and trying not to whimper with desire as his eyes ate her up.

"Maybe you should take me to bed," she started to say as his hand found the sweet spot between her legs again. "Yes." With a sigh of passion, her head rolling back, her eyes closed.

He took advantage of the situation to nibble her ear, suck on her neck, and then drop down to capture her nipple in his hot mouth.

"Oh my," she said as he drew hard on it while teasing her clit with his rough fingertip. Her body started to spasm.

"That's it, babe. Go wild for me." He groaned.

She reached down to unzip his pants with trembling fingers, and gasped when he sprang out hard and ready against her. Commando again, it was enough to drive her into another orgasm as his hot cock thumped against her quivering pussy.

"Nice."

"My thoughts exactly," he said, picking her up so that she was perched over his hard-on. "Yes?" he asked for permission.

She trembled as she looked deep into his passionate dark eyes. "Oh, yes. Take me, cowboy."

She whimpered as he eased her onto his erection, sinking inch by inch onto his rampant cock, until he filled her completely. When they were fully joined, she sighed with pleasure, her heart racing even though, so far, he was doing all the work.

"You're so big and you feel so good inside me."

He groaned like her admission pained him, and she gazed deep into his eyes. "Happy to oblige, darlin'," he gritted.

Frantic for more, she arched her back, taking him deeper, her passion-swollen clit pressing against him, and she cried out in pleasure. He was obviously holding back, trying to be gentle, but she wanted all his wild passion.

"Easy, baby," he said, holding her tightly as he thrust deeper.

Impaled, she could only sob her pleasure as he controlled the thrusts. She was amazed at the strength it took as he held her, thrusting again and again.

"Oh my," she said, clutching his shoulders. She kissed him, their mouths joined as much as their bodies.

His tongue thrust into her mouth in tandem with his cock's thrusts into her pussy, and she dissolved around him into a puddle of need. His shaft rubbed against her G-spot, and she started to quiver, waves of orgasm starting as a ripple, and then completely overtaking her.

He stiffened, his thrusts harder, fiercer, and came high and hard inside her. She clung to him as she fell back to earth, and snuggled against him.

He smoothed a hand up and down her spine, still holding her tight.

Wrapped in the warm cocoon of his arms, she closed her eyes, feeling sated and protected, as a sleepless night caught up with her.

The alarm clock beeping roused Monica from slumber. She opened her eyes, her face pressed against a warm male. She raised her head, her cheek brushing against his stubble-covered chin, and looked into Matt's twinkling blue eyes.

"Good morning, beautiful."

Her face heated. Good morning, indeed. The heady smell of sex in the air mixed with his intoxicating aroma.

"How long have I been...?"

"Sleeping? About an hour." He smiled. "You talk in your sleep."

"When I'm overtired, yeah," she murmured, wondering what she'd said. "I'm sorry for falling asleep on you."

"I'm not, it was a pleasure holding you."

"Thanks," she said, more than flustered. "I have to shower and get ready for work."

He picked her up by the waist, disengaging their bodies, and stood her on her feet. She couldn't help staring as he stood and pulled up his pants. Just the fact that a rampantly endowed man was strutting his stuff around her place was astounding.

"I could wash your back."

"No, thanks. Something tells me I'd be late for work." She backed him toward the front door.

He stopped to look at her, his hand coming up to gently cup and caress her cheek. "Come out to dinner with me tonight, darlin'."

She gazed at him, *yes* on the tip of her tongue, but she had date number one lined up for tonight. It was a blind date. She couldn't break it if she wanted to. Besides, just the inclination she had to chuck her manhunt and settle for a torrid affair was troubling.

"I can't."

"Why not?"

"I have a date." She waited for the usual possessive glare that used to accompany Gary's demands, but it didn't come.

Instead, he nodded dand dropped his hand. "Which guy is it?"

She didn't miss the shrewd look in his eye. He wasn't a jerk like her ex, but guys didn't like to share their toys, which to him, she no doubt was. "Never you mind."

He shrugged. "But we never discussed the shower."

The reminder reinforced the girls' comments about them being too into each other to get down to business last night. "I know. Maybe we could do it over the phone or you could email me."

He shook his head. "How about lunch?"

He wouldn't be easy to shake, and deep down, she was glad of it. She did have extra help in the shop today so she could get away, but could he? She didn't want him to put a construction site on hold just to have lunch with her.

"Don't you have to work?"

"I can juggle things. Well?"

"Swing by Spice at noon and we can walk over to the diner for a quick bite to eat. And, I might suggest you compile a list of ideas."

He glanced at her tote bag sitting on the entry table. "Yeah, the list..."

"See you at noon," she said, quickly shutting the door before he could ask about it.

She leaned against the door, breathing hard. Explaining why she hadn't added him yet wasn't something she wanted to get into. Why hadn't she? Fear? With a groan, she pulled out her notebook and reached for a pencil.

"Pencil him in," he'd said, and that's just what she'd do. But there was nothing to say he couldn't be erased if he broke her heart.

CHAPTER 5

Matt turned into a parking spot behind Spice at quarter to twelve. One glance at Monica's house had him recalling their morning tryst. He'd never known complete passion before. He could still feel her, taste her, wrapped around him, and he wanted more.

Swelling with need, he closed his eyes, and willed his burgeoning erection down. Yeah, right. There wasn't much chance of that. Will had known something was up the minute he'd limped onto the jobsite this morning, but Matt hadn't admitted a thing. Their passion was too new and precious to share, even with his brother.

He got out of his pickup and walked to the back door. There were three other vehicles in the parking lot, one of which was his kid sister's. For once, he was glad she worked here. She freed Monica up to leave with him.

He walked inside, taking off his shades, letting his eyes adjust to the light. There were several shoppers, but he only had eyes for his woman. After their morning delight, he thought of her that way. She was waiting on a customer, so he leaned back against the wall to watch her. She was wearing a green silk blouse that matched her eyes, a black skirt, and another pair of those stilettos that made him so horny.

"Still sticking around the next day," Courtney said with a laugh from somewhere behind him. "That's got to be a record for you, big brother."

He cast a disgruntled look her way as she moved around in front of him while straightening out a rack of lingerie. Blonde and bubbly with laughing blue eyes, his kid sister delighted in needling him. Trouble was, she spoke the truth. He was in trouble if a taste of Monica had him wanting more, but somehow, he didn't care.

Shit, maybe Vegas hadn't taught him a thing. Caution no longer seemed to be part of his vocabulary.

He took a deep breath and waited for the pain that usually accompanied thinking about Tanya, but it didn't come, just a rueful acknowledgement that he'd been stupid. Definite progress, and he had Monica to thank for it.

"We're going out for lunch to discuss the shower."

She smoothed a pink nightgown. "Yeah, I heard you were too busy to do that last night."

Lord, he hoped nothing else about last night had been re-vealed. From Courtney's nosy tone, he could tell she was fishing for information. When she finished her task and turned to face him, he decided the trick was to appease her without revealing anything compromising. Still, having a sister on the inside of the manhunt might help him battle his way to the top of Monica's list.

"Tell me who she's going out with tonight."

Courtney tilted her head as she studied him, then glanced over at Monica. "If she didn't tell you, I'm not sure I should."

He slipped his hands in his pockets trying to look non-jeal-ous. "Why, what do you think I'm gonna do, punch the guy out?"

"No, maybe get your pal Dwain to give him a ticket."

His eyes narrowed at his sister's perceptive statement. He'd thought of it, and about ten other dirty tricks to break up her date, but he'd rejected them all. He didn't want to win her that way.

"I just want to make sure she's okay," he said, meaning every word. Ted Miller's attack last night should have made Monica cautious. Trouble was, he didn't think it had.

"Yeah, she told us about number six's violent behavior last night. Damn the lowlife jerk anyway," Courtney said, worrying her lower lip. She slowly looked him over. "Thanks for saving my boss."

He looked down at his shoes, feeling ill at ease. It'd been a natural reaction. He was no hero, just a man defending his lady. "I should have clobbered the arrogant prick."

"You turned out to be even more of a hero because you didn't have to punch him."

He shrugged. It was the same thing Monica said, and it still didn't figure. Apparently, women appreciated non-violent men. Hell, he'd be a pacifist if it worked.

"So, give, who's she seeing tonight? I want to make sure he's okay."

"Some guy named Don Ormond. One of the customers set her up on a blind date."

"I saw him on the list. The name sounds vaguely familiar, but I can't place him. What do you now about him?"

She shrugged. "Not much. Toni checked him out and he's clean. I do know that Monica wanted to start slow, get her feet wet, so to speak. That's why she put him at the top."

He tried to wipe the jealous look off his face, but from Courtney's wry grin, he knew she wasn't buying it.

"So, the playboy's finally getting a taste of his own medicine," she said with a sad shake of her head.

His first reaction was to give her hell, but she was a casualty in the dating wars, too, after breaking up with her long-term boyfriend a month back. His brotherly advice then that she was better off without the crumb hadn't been well received. Now, the roles were reversed, and he was the one in need of her help.

"I know I didn't say it earlier, but I'm sorry about you and Robert breaking up."

When tears sprang to his sister's eyes, he was bitten by the urge to track rotten Rob down and break him. Instead, he reached out to hug her.

"Thanks," Courtney said, pulling back with a sniff. "I've wasted enough tears on that loser. I guess Dad was right not to trust him."

He smiled, admiring her resilience. "I learned the hard way that we Shepards are keen judges of people when we listen to our instincts, and I can tell you're gonna be okay."

"Yeah, I am, thanks." She glanced at Monica, who was ringing up a sale. "Now, as for your sorry love life, don't worry. I'll keep you in the loop."

He nodded and watched Monica coming their way, poetry in motion, but there was apprehension in her eyes. He could practically feel her pulling away from him. It was as if this morning's sexual surrender hadn't happened. Body tensing, he waited for some sign she wasn't regretting it, that she still wanted him.

She licked her lip. "Mr. Shepard, you're right on time for our business luncheon."

Mr. Shepard? Business luncheon? With his emotions so raw, he frowned at her. Why the formal act? He wasn't about to let her build a wall between them.

Holding eye contact, he pushed away from the wall and sauntered over to her. He watched her eyes widen, heard her quick intake of breath, and knew she hadn't forgotten about this morning any more than he had. It was imprinted on her body and soul, too. Her gaze drifted to his stirring cock, and he relaxed as his hopeful guess was confirmed.

"Ready, Miss Landers?" He touched her arm and felt a tremor go through her. *Ditto, babe*, he thought. Touching her was enough to rock him back on his heels, too. Giving her a little squeeze of reassurance, he let go.

"Let me grab my bag and we can go."

He waited for her to scoop up her tote bag and come back to him. He escorted her the two blocks to the café, reveling in his position at her side. It felt right to be walking together. She smiled as he opened the door for her, and he felt his pride swell along with his cock. One look from her had him primed and ready for action.

Once they were seated in a back booth, he eased back and looked deep into her eyes. She looked a bit tired, despite the catnap she'd caught on his lap this morning. He felt pretty much the same, but the hot sex had helped lift him. At least she didn't have that regretful look in her eyes anymore.

"You look tired, babe. You should go home and rest after lunch." He watched her blush, dart a glance at the mirror behind the counter, and winced, wanting to call back the comment. He'd only mentioned it because he was concerned about her.

"Good grief. Do I really look that bad?"

Smooth, Shepard, he told himself. "No, you look beautiful as always. It's just that I know you didn't get much sleep. Except for an hour this morning, that is."

She fanned her face with the menu and gave him a wry smile. "Ah yes, but they were very restful. Don't worry about me, stud. I'm okay."

He nodded as a weight lifted from his shoulders. At least she was acknowledging their tryst this morning had happened. "Fine."

"Let's talk about the shower, okay?"

He watched, with focused interest, her pull the red leather planner out of her bag. Did she carry it everywhere? What he wouldn't give to take his time pawing through it and learn all her secrets. Something told him pigs would fly first, because it never left her side.

He pulled his wadded up list out of his shirt pocket. "Want to trade?"

To his shock, she actually took him up on the offer, sliding her planner over and reaching for his list. She smoothed out the crumpled paper. He watched her arch a perfect brow as she read his short list.

"You want us to plan a couple's shower?"

He shrugged, a bit insulted by her shock. Her low evaluation of his sophistication level stung, hitting a little too close to home. It reminded him of Tanya's parting words, that she'd rather sip champagne with his boss Joe Falcon than drink beer with him, as he lay broken in the street after Falcon's goons had roughed him up. At the time, it was just insult added to the injury of his professional and personal demise. Now, to hear something similar coming from Monica stung, even though he knew she didn't intend it as a put down. He wasn't completely tasteless, even if he worked with his hands.

"Why not? It's the latest thing, isn't it?"

"Well, yes, but not around here. I didn't think construction workers would want to party with the ladies."

"We're not all Neanderthals."

"Besides, I figured you'd want a stripper at Red's."

He knew that jab was aimed mostly at him, but the idea of a stripper didn't do anything for him anymore. Tame stuff compared to the sultry woman across from him.

"Who, me?"

She shrugged. "Okay, a couple's shower it is. We can have separate bridal shower and bachelor party, too."

"Sure, I'm easy." He leaned back and smiled at her.

She gave him a wry look. "Well, that was fast. See what we can do when other things don't get in the way?"

"So, did you add me to the list?"

Monica froze, Matt's abrupt question catching her by surprise. First, she'd unintentionally hurt his feelings with her comments about the couple's shower. She could see it in the way he'd tensed and acted distracted, as if he wasn't really with her anymore. And now, he wanted to know his place in her life when she really didn't know herself. The need to protect herself ran too deep to be hasty.

"Um, yeah, in a way," she stammered, stalling.

Her heart skipped a beat when he flipped a few pages to look. His name was there, all right, but scrawled across the bottom in pencil. The fact that she'd erased him twice only to reenter him was obvious from the smears. How would he take it? She stared at him, noting he'd grown silent and stiff like he was bracing for battle.

"What gives? I'm only written in pencil."

"Well, you did say 'pencil me in.'" He seemed more disappointed than angry, and it broke through her defenses like nothing else could. He was unlike any other man she'd met, and she simply didn't know how to handle him.

"You're right. I did, but you didn't have to take me so literally."

The urge to chuck her manhunt and fall completely under his spell was so strong, she could barely control it. Only the memory of how foolish she'd been when she let her heart lead before kept her from acting on it. Matt was worlds away from Gary, but he was still a player.

"I'm sorry, Matthew. I never meant to hurt your feelings."

He shrugged, brushing off her mention of his ruffled feathers. "Tell me about your date tonight."

She went still, giving him a wary glance. She'd had a feeling the subject would come up. "Why do you want to know?" She watched him smile, trying to come off more like a friend than a jealous lover, but she didn't buy it.

"I'm just looking out for you, darlin'," he said with a frown. "You can't have a replay of last night's assault."

Nonplussed, she took in Matt's repressive frown in an annoyed glance. Didn't her moves last night prove she could protect herself in his eyes? She'd handled Ted Miller, admittedly with a little backup from Matt, but she could have done him in herself if she had to. She'd been studying martial arts since Gary had been imprisoned, for just such an occasion.

"I haven't needed a babysitter since I was six. I fended that loser off just like I will the next one. Since when are you my bodyguard, Shepard?"

"Maybe since I saved your ass and slept with you."

The calmly stated words threw her so bad, she could only gape at him for a moment, hardly believing they'd come out of his sensual mouth. The fact she knew it was true only made it worse. His solid presence, his big hand enfolding hers, gave her no way to deny they were involved. She wanted to climb over the table and curl up in his lap, but instead, she had to reassert her independence.

"I took care of the last guy, and I'll take care of the next. I don't need you or any other man to do it for me." She pulled her hand out from under his. "No guy's ever going to have the power to threaten me again."

He frowned. "Who's threatened you?"

When she remained silent, he seethed.

"I'm worried about you, not trying to boss you around. Yes, you might have gotten away unscathed, but think about the next time, babe. I shudder to think what might happen."

His confession defused the situation, and she let out a sigh. It felt good to know he cared, even if she didn't want to be owned. "Don't worry about me. We've come up with an early warning system if I should have any trouble."

"We? Who else is in on this mess?"

She didn't much like the way he said *mess*, but she decided to overlook it. "My posse, the Bridesmaid Manhunter's Club."

"Good Lord." He groaned and closed his eyes. "What's the plan?"

She licked her lip, hesitating as she watched him, then sighed. "I'm going to carry my cell phone at all times. Courtney will call me at eight, and I can come up with an excuse to leave the date early if he turns out to be boring or worse. Also, if I get into trouble, I can send text messages to my friends. Don't forget, I've got a friend on the force. Toni's been vetting my dates, and we haven't dug up any dirt on number one yet."

"That's it." He frowned. "Toni's fairly new on the force, and while she might be good at her job, it's not enough backup in case of trouble. Care for a chauffer?"

"No! There's no way you're coming along. You'd probably drop the poor guy off in the woods and take me parking instead."

"Sounds like an excellent idea," he said with a grin.

"Down, boy," she said, smiling ruefully back at him. "It's not going to happen."

"If not me, take Toni. She can probably get the night off, and the sight of her is liable to cool his jets."

"Hey, I resent that. Toni is very pretty."

"Yeah, if you go for redheaded elves who carry guns."

"She's not an elf, she's just petite. And she's very fond of that gun, and a crack shot, to boot."

"So, all the more reason to take her along. The guy could be an axe murderer for all you know."

She rolled her eyes, because there was no reasoning with him. "First of all, I expect the evening to go off without a hitch, as it's my first real foray into manhunting. Second, if anything should go wrong, I've got my mace."

He closed his eyes and slumped back in his seat. "Good God."

CHAPTER 6

Monica smoothed the wrinkles out of her cream linen skirt and slipped on her lightweight pink cashmere twin set, hoping to look presentable but unavailable as she got ready for her date.

Matt's words of warning still rang in her ears from their lunch this afternoon. He was making her paranoid, a state she was quite familiar with because of Gary, who'd robbed her, and been verbally abusive during their short marriage. But he hadn't actually laid a hand on her until their last confrontation. When he'd realized she'd turned him in, he'd snapped and damned near choked the life out of her before he was hauled away. She was strong and prepared now, so it could never happen again.

She checked the tote bag to make sure her cell phone and mace were in place. It didn't pay to take any chances. The manhunt would continue, but under her terms. Number one was due to pick her up any minute, and he had quite a few hurdles to cross over before he even got to hold her hand. This morning's crazy love liaison determinedly thrust into the back of her mind, she would return to the task of finding a husband.

Don sounded perfect on paper. A former classmate, she remembered him as the sweet, quiet type of guy, who was said to be a successful CPA. He'd just recently moved back home, so there weren't any local entanglements to get in the way. A customer who was a friend of a friend had set up this blind date, and she only hoped it would meet with success. Anything to take her mind off Sundance, and refocus it on her goals.

Matt was only penciled in for a reason. She expected to have to erase him soon. He wasn't really marriage minded. As soon as he tired of the chase, he'd move on to his next conquest and drop her. The fact that the thought made her crazy was demoralizing. She'd been through tough times before. She just had to stay strong.

Don's car pulled into her driveway, and she grabbed her tote. The bell rang, and she opened the door to Don on her doorstep. He looked pretty much like she remembered from high school, only older. His brown hair was starting to recede, his light blue eyes were lined with crow's feet in his ultra tanned face, but his smile was friendly. It was his outfit that stopped her short—a checked sports jacket with pinstriped pants. She couldn't help staring. It was a designer's nightmare. Shorter than Matt, he was at her eye level.

Great, now she'd taken to comparing others to Matt. *Get back in the game girl*, she told herself.

"Hi."

"Ready to go, Mo?"

She tried not to cringe at the hated nickname. "I sure am."

She locked her door and walked beside him to his SUV. When he reached for her elbow, she flinched, gun-shy, but luckily, he didn't comment. She couldn't help noticing he didn't open her door. Ever the liberated woman, she didn't comment, just tugged open her door and got in.

"Where to?"

He turned to smile at her as he started the car. "I was thinking dinner and a movie. How about Italian?"

"Sounds good to me. I love Italian."

Matt stood at the bar at Red's, waiting for his table's drink order, unable to think about anything but Monica out with another man. He was jealous, a revelation to him. Since when did "love them and leave them" him get hooked this bad? Since he'd met Monica, of course. It wasn't just jealousy. He felt a healthy dose of concern, as well. He'd done some digging about this Don Ormond guy, and hadn't been able to find anything, either. In a small town like Landis Falls, where everyone knows everyone else's business, that was saying something.

He picked up the tray of beverages and carried it over to the table where Courtney, April, and Will were eating pizza. He handed Courtney her diet cola, planning to stick like glue to her side as a way to keep tabs on Monica. It was his only way to make sure she was safe.

Someone passed him a piece of pizza, but he didn't touch it. Instead, he looked at the clock. Only quarter to eight.

"Why don't you call her?" he said to Courtney.

"It's not time yet. Boy, you've got it bad." Courtney chuckled.

"Lay off," Will scolded, then turned to Matt. "So, did you find out anything about the guy?"

"Zilch, not so much as a parking ticket."

Courtney nodded. "That's what Toni said."

"I don't like it." Matt frowned and looked at the clock.

"That's also what Toni said, but then she tends to shoot first and ask questions later."

Monica picked at her lasagna as Don wolfed down his, then started in on his glass of Chianti. So far, their date had been as exciting as watching paint dry. Still, she owed it to him to get to know him better before she rejected him out of hand.

She put down her fork. "So, tell me about your life, Don. We kind of lost touch since high school."

He set aside his empty wine glass and gazed at her cleavage. "Not much to tell, really. I got my MBA and joined an accounting firm, and then a few months back, I decided to move home."

She couldn't help noticing the way his gaze stayed locked on her boobs instead of her face, and bristled. *You aren't getting any of this pal, so put your googly eyes back in your head.*

"So, you never settled down with someone special?" she said, making small talk and watching his gaze dull. Obviously, talk of love and marriage wasn't in his vocabulary. Time to move onto number two, fast.

"Well, as a matter of fact, I've been married, but it didn't work out."

She was almost surprised to hear that a guy as icky as him had found someone to marry. "Oh, sorry to hear that."

"Yeah, things were tough for a while, but they're better now that I'm living with my mother."

Now the mismatched clothes made sense. Mom must be doing his laundry. Only a mom would pair checks and stripes. She tried not to cringe.

"You moved back home with your mom?"

"Sure, it's perfect. She's got someone to fuss over and I don't have to hire a housekeeper. It works for me. If I want to get cozy with a woman, I go to her place."

She didn't miss his leer when he said *get cozy*. Repulsed, she frowned at him, but he didn't seem to notice...because he was staring at her breasts. Did all men think her a slut? All but Matt, was the answer. Her phone rang, and she couldn't help noticing

Don's irritated scowl as she fished it out of her tote bag. Bad form, maybe, but it could be her saving grace.

"Sorry, this could be business related. I'll just take it in the foyer."

"Take your time, toots. I'm not going anywhere."

Wincing, she knew she was stuck with him as she slipped out of the dining room, flipped open her phone, and made tracks for the empty hostess section. "Hi."

"How goes it?" Courtney asked.

"Not very good," she murmured. But was she really giving him a fair chance? What man could live up to Matt? "But not that bad, either."

"So, you don't need me to send in the cavalry?"

Monica closed her eyes, picturing her Manhunter's Club descending on them en mass. Don would go back to his mom's and never come out. He might be icky, but she couldn't do that to him, even if he was dull as dishwater.

"I don't think so. If he's hard to shake and I need to cut things short, I'll text you to ring me back, okay?"

"You sure about this? I can be there in five minutes."

"I'm sure. Just because he isn't the man of my dreams doesn't mean I should be impolite." Listening to the jangle of a jukebox and a certain male voice in the background, Monica had a sinking feeling. She plopped onto the nearest chair. "He's there, isn't he?"

"Yeah, we're all here at Red's eating pizza. He's not trying to be a pest, he's just worried about you."

"And possessive, too," Monica murmured.

"That, too. You're not mad, are you?"

Monica sighed, clutching the phone tight. Mad? Yes. Also frustrated, bedazzled, and ready to tell Don to take a hike so she can climb through the phone to get to Matt. "No, I know it's genuine."

"He's the real deal, all right. I guess my big brother is hard to live up to, huh?"

What an understatement. "I'm afraid so." She was touched by the fact he was trying to look out for her, even though it meant he didn't believe she could take care of herself. "Tell him not to worry, okay. Don might bore me to death, but he's perfectly harmless."

She sighed, hung up, and made her way back to the table.

Don set down a glass of wine at her approach. "Is everything okay?"

"It's fine, just a question about inventory."

"Ready to go?" he asked, standing.

"Sure." Her hopes lifted. Soon, she'd be home, tucked into bed alone, and able to dream about Matt.

He took her elbow and weaved her toward the door. "If you want to bag the movie and go check on things, I wouldn't mind, Mo. It'd give me a chance to check the place out. What I've heard sounds intriguing." He waggled his brow at her as he led her out into the parking lot.

She cringed at the thought, but thankfully, the valet pulled up with Don's SUV, and she was spared the task of dousing his ardor.

He went around to the driver's side door, leaving her alone.

She opened her own door and got in, grateful this date was almost over. "No, thanks. In fact, I've got a headache. I'd like to go home."

He grinned and gunned the engine, taking off. "I get the message. Sure, toots, we'll go back to your place."

The aroma of stale wine wafted through the car as he spoke. How many glasses had he downed while she was on the phone? Too many, if it gave him this much liquid courage.

"I don't think you should drive."

"Bullshit. I'm fine," he grumbled, turning onto the highway.

She sat there in stunned silence as he turned from pathetic mamma's boy to reckless drunk driver. It was too late to stop him or leap out without hurting herself. She fished her phone out of her bag and pushed Courtney's number.

"Hey," he snarled, taking a wild swipe at her phone, but missing. "No cell phones in my car. I've got to think of my insurance, stupid broad."

She shrunk back, pulled her phone out of his line of sight, and hung up just as Courtney answered. "Okay. Now, how about you pull over and let me drive?"

"Sorry," he said with a chuckle. "No broad drives my car, toots. But don't worry, I got something else you can drive later."

Eww! She eased over a little farther, and keeping her cell phone hidden, sending a text. "Come on, Don, you're drunk. Pull over and let me drive."

"No way. Now you sound like my ex-wife." He swiveled his head to scowl at her, the car swerving. "I didn't think you'd be that kind of tight-assed bitch."

She gasped as the car skittered toward the ditch, and she reached for her mace. He was going to kill somebody.

A siren went off behind them and lights flashed.

Her shoulders sagged with relief. Toni to the rescue.

"God damn it," Don grumbled as he straightened out the swerve and pulled to the shoulder of the road, stopping the vehicle. "Keep your mouth shut, woman, and I'll get us out of this."

She quickly unfastened her seatbelt, preparing to bolt. No way would she spend another second in his obnoxious presence. She looked over her shoulder to find Dwain Carter bearing down on them. Six-foot, four of surly police officer, he was no one to mess with. She almost felt sorry for Don. Almost.

There was a tap on her window. Toni hunkered at her side, spiky red hair poking out from her police cap, and Monica had a vast sense of relief.

She opened her door and bailed.

"You okay?" Toni asked.

"I am now." She squeezed Toni's hand.

"Hey, where ya going?" Don called.

Dwain pinned them with a serious gaze over the hood of the car. "She okay, partner?"

Toni nodded.

"*Partner?*" Monica mouthed with surprise, and grinned when hard-edged Toni actually blushed.

Dwain looked back at Don. "License and registration, sir."

"But I haven't done anything wrong, officer," Don whined. "Don't listen to the crazy broad. I'm not drunk."

"Come on," Toni urged Monica back to the squad car. "We don't need a front row seat for this."

Monica trailed after her feeling like an idiot for her bad taste in men. *Except for Matt*, a little voice in her head said. Two possible mates shot down in two days. She stood by Toni's side, watching Don take a Breathalyzer test, and wanted to scream. The past two days had been an emotional roller coaster. It was embarrassing as cars slowed to gawk.

The radio started to squawk, and Toni leaned in to answer it. She came out grim-faced a moment later, muttering, "He's got priors, with an alias from another state. Damn, why didn't I pick up on it?"

She walked toward Dwain to tell him. She came back, and a moment later, Don was sprawled over the hood of his car and handcuffed.

Toni frowned. "He's being taken in for three DWI's in a year under another name, and he's got priors for being in nonsupport from out of state. It seems there are two ex-wives looking for him."

"Oh Lord." It was even worse than Monica thought. "And number one bites the dust. Another evening shot to hell."

Toni looked over her shoulder. "Maybe not."

Monica was startled by the amusement in her friend's voice. There was nothing remotely funny about this disaster. She turned to look in the same direction, and groaned.

Matt was striding their way with a pissed off glint in his eyes. He glared at Don as he was placed in the back of the squad car, and then his concerned gaze fell on her.

"What did the dirtbag do to you? I'll kill him."

"Settle down, boy. He's being taken in for DWI and resisting arrest. You're welcome." Toni walked to the passenger side of the patrol car.

CHAPTER 7

Matt tried to keep his cool. He hadn't really planned to interfere with her date, just keep tabs on her through Courtney to make sure she was okay. Monica's cut-off call and then her panicked text message made his blood run cold, and knew things had gone dangerously sour. Now, seeing her standing, trembling on the side of the road, her arms wrapped protectively around herself, it was all he could do not to wrap her up in cotton wool and drive her back to his place. Instead, he tried to read her gloomy expression. She was angry, but maybe not with him. The fact she wasn't chewing him out gave him hope.

"It looks like your first date is over."

"Yeah, we never even got to the movies, and number one is toast. It looks like the manhunt system needs revamping." She shrugged, then cast a lingering look his way. "On the plus side, you keep coming to my rescue, Sundance."

He felt like laughing when she actually smiled at him. Tension rolled off him as he stepped closer. "Hey, at least I'm good for something."

He held his breath when she casually linked her arm with his, sending raw heat clear through him.

"You're good for lots of things."

He tugged her close to his side as a wrecker pulled away with Don's SUV. Her lush body pressed against his made it hard for him to think, but he forced himself to focus.

Clearing his throat he offered, "Still want to go to the show? I'll take you."

"Actually, I've got a better idea," she murmured.

"And what's that?" he asked, gazing into her sultry eyes as her soft hand ran up his bare forearm. He watched the corners of her sexy mouth kick up in a playful grin, and wanted to shout out his delight.

She licked her lip. "Well, we never did make it to bed this morning."

Heart racing, he nodded. He could hardly believe his dumb luck, but he wasn't going to question it. There had to be a wild angel looking after him to put her in his bed after this mess.

"You're right, darlin'. Let's go." Taking her arm, he hurried her toward his truck, asking, "My place or yours?"

Monica rushed to keep up with Matt as he took her on a dead run to his pickup truck. She couldn't help being a bit surprised by his haste. Didn't he know how irresistible she found him? She was bonkers about him, and even more now that he'd come to her rescue again. She'd known he was with Courtney tonight, and knew he'd eventually find out about this debacle, but she hadn't actually figured on him swooping in to save her.

"Which is closer?" she asked as he jerked open her truck door.

"Yours. I have a ranch out in the country."

The disclosure didn't surprise her. He was a cowboy.

"Then, let's go to my place," she said, starting to clamber inside.

She let out a startled gasp when he picked her up by the waist and all but plopped her onto the bench seat, giving a whole new meaning to 'pickup'. She giggled, earning a frown from him as he pushed her door shut. She watched him sprint around to the driver's side, the streetlight highlighting his handsome face and his fluid strength as he moved.

Ogling him in admiration, she started heating up as he climbed in, gunned the engine, and drove them toward her house. Now that she had him at her side, there was no question about her holding on tight for the night. She wouldn't have the strength to let go.

Her senses were on high alert. She could actually feel the charged particles between them as she took in a deep breath of his musky, all-male scent and inched closer. Her hands itched to start stripping the shirt off him now. She tucked them under her legs to make them behave. Making love in her bed? Now that had possibilities.

They pulled into the parking space in front of her house, and she stopped fantasizing. Time for the real thing. At least for tonight, she had her Sundance. Her hands trembled as she unfastened her seatbelt. Matt was already out of the truck and had her door open as she turned toward him.

"This way to paradise, darlin'," he said, tugging her out of the vehicle.

She gasped as he slowly lowered her to the ground, letting her body slide down his, until she was standing on wobbling heels. She slumped against him, getting wet in anticipation. His nearness was making her crazy, needy, in love.

Scratch that. She wouldn't think in terms of love.

Pushing away before she did something crazy, like strip him naked in the parking lot, she focused on pulling her keys out of her bag, making them clink because she was trembling.

"Let me." His hand covered hers.

She moaned when his big hand enveloped hers. He took the keys and brought her hand to his mouth to press a kiss to her palm. She melted, getting wetter. Holding her hand, he walked her up to her front door, and quickly unlocked it.

He turned to give her back her keys, but she ignored them, kissing him instead. He let out a groan, leaning against her doorframe and adopting a wide stance so that she could step between his legs. Pressing against him, she deepened the kiss, her body on fire for him. She rubbed her tingling nipples against him, sighing with pleasure while he growled.

Oh yeah, he had what it took to satisfy, and turn her love life around.

She half-pushed, half-urged him over the threshold, and he let out a sexy chuckle that made her kind of crazy. The fact that she couldn't hide her sexuality from him didn't bother her. He kicked shut the door and she pressed against him, scattering kisses over his face. Things were fast moving out of control, and for once in her life, she didn't mind a bit. His arms were around her, his big hands stroking her back, cupping her ass as he pulled her tight to his erection, letting her feel how involved he truly was.

Ablaze, she pressed kisses against his neck, his chin, feeling his body grow even harder against hers as his burgeoning cock pushed against her. He was just as turned on. Snuggling, she sucked on his neck, his breathing growing ragged.

"Which way to the bedroom, darlin'?"

She sort of waved her hand in a direction, dizzy with desire. A moment later, he scooped her up in his strong arms, which made her even dizzier. It all seemed like a wild erotic dream, and she reached out to pinch him to make sure he was real.

"Hey," he said with a chuckle.

She smiled at him, memorizing his face. It wasn't every day a girl got swept off her feet by a sex god. "Just checking to make sure you're real, Sundance."

"I'll prove it to you," he said, striding into her bedroom.

Still in his arms, she looked around her bedroom, dazzled to have him in it. She glanced at her double bed. Was he too tall? "Do you think you'll fit?"

"Like a glove." He set her on her feet with a kiss.

She didn't need to hear more. She shrugged her cashmere cardigan off and then pulled off her shell. His warm eyes eating her up emboldened her. She reached back to unzip her skirt and let it drop to the floor with a thump. Suddenly, she stood there in only her bra, panties, and high heels. She was so glad she'd opted for the burgundy satin when his appreciative glance swept over her. She stood there for a few seconds, surveying her prize. Just looking at him made her heart beat faster.

He cocked a grin. "I await your pleasure, my lady."

She prowled over to him, hearing his amused tone, but it didn't put her off. It was time to take charge. Stepping into his personal space, anticipation surged through her. Her pussy was quivering, her nipples were tingling, and he hadn't even touched her yet. There was some kind of strange magic about him. She reached up to unbutton his shirt. Her eyes met his, and she promptly got lost in their hypnotic blue depths.

Forcing herself to slow down, she insisted, "I want you, Matthew, but under my conditions."

"Of course."

His instant capitulation wasn't convincing, especially considering the huge bulge in his pants and the heated look in his eyes. She knew he was patronizing her, but she was too needy to stop.

"Just so you understand."

Tugging off his shirt with trembling hands, she leaned forward to nibble on his neck. His body jerked and he let out a low groan the instant her lips touched him.

"Whatever you say, lady."

Satisfied, she reached down to unzip his jeans. His cock sprang out into her hands. He was already hard and huge, and she couldn't resist giving him a little squeeze. He groaned and surged into her hands, like hot, velvet-covered steel. Just as overcome, she licked her lips. He was going commando again, and she idly wondered if she could break him of it. For a lingerie designer to go with a guy who spurned underwear...

"Really, Shepard, don't you ever wear underwear?"

Chuckling dryly, he arched his hips, thrusting himself firmly into her hands. "Do you mind?"

"Not really," she was forced to admit, as she felt his power. "Maybe I should design a men's line," she mused out loud, giving him another little squeeze.

He bit back a groan, saying, "Babe, if you ever need a man to measure for them, I'm him."

"I might just hold you to that," she said with a smile.

Holding the full length of his hot cock in her hand was enough to make her reach for her Good Head Gel. But then he distracted her by deftly unhooking her bra. Startled by the quick movement, she realized she wasn't completely in charge, after all. A smart woman who stuck to her guns would object. After all, hadn't he just agreed to let her set the pace? Instead, she looked into his eyes and melted. She let the bra slip off, and tossed it on the floor, feeling sexy as he just stood and gazed at her for a long moment. Her nipples hardened before his very eyes and she arched toward him like a flower to the sun. They needed his attention. *She* needed his attention, bad.

She let out a needy whimper. "Please."

"Oh, darlin', I will," he murmured. His work-roughened fingers came up to shape and roll her sensitive nipples, tugging on them, lengthening them.

She closed her eyes in bliss as she leaned toward him, thrusting them out for his loving attention.

"Got anymore of the strawberry gel?"

Her eyes popped open at the unexpected question. "In my bag."

He picked up the bag from the floor and rifled through it, frowning at the planner, before pulling out the half-empty tube.

Her mouth watered in anticipation. Did he want her to go down on him again? The question was answered a moment later when he opened the tube and squeezed a dollop on her right nipple. She whimpered at the horny cold/hot, then he bent to take her budded nipple into his mouth. She let out a cry as he drew her tingling strawberry peak hard into his hot mouth. Her knees went weak as she leaned against him.

He pressed her back against the armoire, thrust his thigh between her legs to hold her up, and kept on sucking. She ground her panty-clad pussy against his hard leg, her eyes rolling back in her head at the exquisite twin sensations. He kept drawing harder on her nipple, sucking and nipping, his rough tongue laving the tortured peak. From seemingly out of nowhere, she felt a dollop of cold gel on her other nipple.

She let out a helpless whimper when he gave that one a good-bye kiss and moved on to the right. She stiffened in anticipation, so on fire, she didn't know if she could handle it. Her pussy was throbbing, quivering against his thigh, as her abdomen tightened with need. Her gel-covered nipple burned with ice as she waited what seemed like forever for him to take it in his mouth. Instead, he blew on it.

"Oh," she cried as a heat wave drew it tighter, and then his mouth closed over it.

Shivering, grinding against him as little mewling noises poured out of her mouth at the double arousal, empty spasms fluttered through her pussy. She stiffened, crying out as she came, and came, and came.

Moments later, he released her nipple with a little kiss to its tip.

She sagged against him, spent, but not really satisfied as he held her. She closed her eyes, comforted by his strong arms. He held her for a few moments, then picked her up like she weighed no more than a limp rag doll. She wrapped herself around him, her arms around his neck, her legs around his waist, as her high heels dropped off one by one. The moment her open pussy pressed against his washboard abs, the tingling of arousal returned, and she realized this wasn't over by a long shot.

His hands, cupping her ass, squeezed, and she let out a little giggle.

"Are you fixing to ride me, cowboy?"

"What do you think?" he asked, holding her in a secure grip as he carried her to the bed. He gently laid her down, then quickly stripped off the rest of his clothes, his eyes never leaving hers.

She lay still on the bed, watching him. Neither one of them could look away. If they did, it might all disappear. He came back to the bed, his hot gaze making her burn, as he reached for her panties. She arched her hips off the bed as he started to slowly peel them down, feeling like a virgin sacrifice even though she was no innocent. Everything was new with Matthew, even the simple business of getting naked. When she was bare to his gaze, she lay exposed, basking in his obvious delight. It felt so right to have this man think she was special.

"Perfect," he whispered.

Knowing he meant the words opened up a piece of her heart she'd kept guarded.

He picked up the Good Head Gel, and she trembled.

No more nipple play, it felt good, but she needed him inside her now. "Oh, please."

His mouth kicked up in a knowing grin. Instead of aiming for her nipples, he squeezed a line of gel onto her bare pussy, putting an extra dollop on her swollen clit.

Panting, she let out a little screech of surprise. So Good Head could be just as useful on women. It was a great promotional tip, but then, all thoughts of business flew away when he knelt between her quivering thighs and flicked a long stroke of his rough tongue up her pussy. With a cry of delight, she arched toward that tantalizing tongue. Trembling, she lost count of the teasing strokes. He sucked the swollen nub of her clit into his hot mouth. Her eyes rolled back in her head as she began to contract.

"Oh yes, yes, yes," she screamed as she came.

With a growl, he surged up her trembling body and thrust his stiff cock into her contracting pussy, simultaneously claiming her mouth with a kiss. She tasted her essence, strawberries, and him all at the same time, and was hit with sensory overload. He pulled almost completely out of her, and slammed back in to the hilt. She was ready for the sensual assault, needed it, as she snapped her hips up to meet his fevered thrusts. Kissing, loving, she felt like one big erogenous zone as her clit rubbed against his pelvis.

She wrapped her legs around his hips, trapping him to her as her body shook. Deep spasms tugged him inside her as her pleasure peaked. Waves of orgasm exploded, and she saw stars behind her closed eyelids.

He thrust into her once more and went still, pouring out his tribute.

He rolled them over so that her limp body lay atop his and she was astride him.

She sighed with completion as his big hands stroked her back. Wrapped around him, she felt like she wanted to stay that way forever. A few moments later, she felt him stirring again.

She looked at him, surprised. "Again?"

He chuckled and picked up her bunny from the nightstand. "Look what I found."

She smiled as he switched it on. "Just what do you think you're going to do with that?"

"How about this." He brushed it teasingly across her left nipple.

She cried out at the pleasure, arching her hips against him. Heavens, that felt good! He moved on to the other peak, teasing it. She was trembling, moaning, when he slipped it down to buzz her clit. She lifted up a tiny bit to give him access. He kept thrusting his cock into her and buzzing her clit, sending sparks of desire through her.

"You are amazing."

He groaned, thrusting deeper. "That's it, darlin', take me."

She gasped. Her swollen clit pressed against the vibrator while his cock stretched her pussy as she sat up, impaled on his once more hard cock. Starting slow, she gradually increased in speed, until she was trembling, contracting around him. He made love to her. He was so big, and deep inside her. Her head fell back, and she moaned, ripples of pleasure fluttered through her as she started to come.

He simultaneously grasped her hip tightly with one hand, driving her down to take him completely, while moving the vibrator to her anus. She screamed, coming harder, feeling surrounded by him, taken at all sides. He grasped her hips, holding her as he thrust deep into her again and again. She sobbed with release as she met his fierce thrusts. Rippling spasms rocked her pussy and ass, little explosions going off deep inside her as she came like she'd never come before. Now she knew why people indulged in anal sex, but she'd only had a taste of it. Clinging to him, she convulsed, all thought vanishing as her orgasm pulled him deeper, tugging at his cock as she cried out. He held her against him, thrusting high, inside, and exploding with a growl of delight.

"*My* darlin'," he growled.

She felt warmed by the claim of possession, even though it went against her rules. Bathed in the afterglow, she sprawled on top of his hard muscular chest, listening to his thundering heartbeat slow.

She lifted her head and smiled at him.

"That was—"

"Amazing," she completed, cuddling close to him.

"Amazing fits. I was going to say crazy hot."

"That, too. I think you found a way to spice up the bunny experience."

Chuckling, he held her tight.

Reveling in the warm feeling, she thought how right it felt to be in his arms. "This is nice."

"Just about perfect, but..."

"But what?" she asked, wrinkling her nose against his resilient chest. He was growing tense, his muscles stiffening against her cheek.

"You don't seem to agree," he finished.

His suddenly reserved tone disturbed her almost as much as his words. Just what was he getting at? "I never said that."

"Then, you do consider me more than a one-night-stand?"

The question shocked her and made her try to sit up in bed, but he kept hold of her. It was gentle, but it was still a restraint. The time had come for her to reluctantly reassert her independence. But then his warm hand stroked her back, soothing her, and she snuggled close to him.

He was feeling insecure.

She could relate. "Of course, you're more than a one-night-stand."

"Then, we're officially..."

"Dating," she cut in before he could press her for more than she was willing to give.

"And the manhunt?"

She placed a kiss above his nipple, which budded at the contact. "I have a date tomorrow night." She waited for any objection. None came, but there was a slight hesitation in her backrub.

"Okay. I can handle a little competition. I just want a place in your life."

She smiled, feeling a vast sense of relief. It was all working out. She'd have her hunk, as long as he chose to stay with her, and her manhunt. "Okay, I guess I can handle dating as long as there are no strings attached."

CHAPTER 8

The next night, Monica sat next to Ed Flanagan on a blanket in the park at the city's band concert, bored to tears. At least the band kept them from carrying on a stilted one-sided conversation on auto mechanics, which happened to be Ed's passion as well as his profession. Number two was no doubt sorry he'd asked her out, and the feeling was mutual. It wasn't his fault. She simply couldn't keep her mind on him. She was too busy thinking about Matt, who she hadn't seen since he'd left her bed with a morning kiss.

What was he doing tonight? He'd said something about a business dinner, and she couldn't help but wonder who he was with and where? What if he met some woman who put the moves on him? He was under no requirement to be faithful to her. After all, she was out with another man, even though nothing intimate would ever happen between Ed and her. She was the one who'd insisted on no strings attached, and now it was coming back to haunt her.

Ed applauded at the end of the music, and it roused her out of her musings. They were almost as dark as the scudding clouds above. She shivered as the wind picked up and pulled her wrap snug around her shoulders. It looked like rain coming in. Sitting under an oak tree in the middle of an oncoming thunderstorm might be tempting fate. Fortunately, the concert was ending.

Ed got to his feet and politely extended a hand to help her up.

As she stood, a flash of movement across the street caught her eye.

Matt, dressed in faded jeans and a leather jacket, walked out of a café with a pretty redhead on his arm.

Monica's heart sank as she watched Chandra Ellison cling to his side, laughing at something he'd said. Jealousy and despair surged through her as she watched the pretty massage therapist, a frequent shopper at Spice, seem to hang on his every word. Matt smiled back at her as he handed her a key.

Monica stood, rooted to the spot, as pain turned to outrage. All his sweet talk about wanting to be on the manhunt had been just that. Talk.

"Are you feeling okay, Monica? You look kind of green about the gills." Ed looked at her curiously.

Matt went still, and then spun to look in their direction. He frowned at them, Chandra still at his side.

She couldn't find her voice, couldn't seem to move as her heart shattered. She should confront him, have it out, and get it over with. A quick break was easiest, but something told her it wouldn't ever be easy with him.

Just as she made her mind up to move, Matt strode toward her, towing Chandra in his wake. "Ed, hold up a minute."

Ed let go of Monica's arm and turned to Matt. "Hey, Shepard, long time no see. How's it going? When you going to bring that sweet truck of yours in for a tune up? I been dying to get my hands on her."

"How about next week?" Matt turned his focus on Monica. "Darlin', I wasn't expecting to run into you here."

"Obviously not," she said, cutting a pointed look to Chandra, still clinging to Matt's arm. "It looks like we both got caught with our hands in the cooking jar."

His scowl deepened, and she wondered about it. Why the offended look? He'd been caught red-handed, or had he? Was it possible Chandra was his business dinner? She'd heard something about Chandra building a new spa. Confused, she tried to ignore Chandra's amused glance, but it wasn't easy. Jealousy sucked.

"Maybe one of us did, but it wouldn't be me." He tugged Chandra forward. "Meet my business dinner companion, Chandra Ellison. Ace Builders just finished construction on Essence Day Spa."

"We know each other," Chandra cut in. "Did you ever get that new shipment of teddies in, honey?"

Face flushing, Monica managed to nod awkwardly. "Sure, stop by next week, and they'll be there."

"Great," Chandra said before turning to Matt. "Well, stud, thanks for the key. Now that we've concluded our business, I think I'll be on my way." She dangled the shiny gold key from her finger. "One week early and under budget. You do good work, boyfriend." She reached up to give him a kiss on the cheek.

Monica stood there, burning with chagrin and embarrassment. It was a business dinner, but the woman's familiarity still bugged her. Matt, for his part, seemed unperturbed, like having women throw themselves at him was normal.

Sighing, she decided that it was. He was every woman's wet dream. When they parted company, she couldn't help musing that maybe it was time to table her manhunt and play this one out.

Matt walked up to Spice after five the next evening, feeling tense. On the plus side, he hadn't made an ass of himself last night when he'd spied Ed holding Monica's hand. Also, he'd gotten a reaction out of Monica that told him he actually meant more to her than a casual lay. Best of all, he'd kept his word to let her carry out her manhunt. He hadn't acted on his urge to follow her home and make love to her until she couldn't even look at another man.

Unfortunately, he hadn't expected to bump into Monica with Chandra at his side. After banging off a work list of nit-picky items she'd vacillated on for weeks, he was relieved to be finally rid of her. She might be a childhood friend, but as a client, she was a royal pain.

It was after eight, and the closed sign was hanging in the window, so he and Monica could shop for party favors for the couple's shower. He tapped on the back door and waited what seemed like an eternity for her to let him in. He was more than anxious to see her. Would she be angry? He'd unintentionally showed her that two could play the field, but it might just come back to bite him in the ass.

He'd know in about two seconds as he heard her high heels clicking toward the door. His gut tightened as he waited while she undid the lock and pulled open the door.

Monica stood on the other side looking good enough to eat. She was nervous, he could tell by the stiff set of her shoulders, but at least she wasn't throwing things at him. He stepped over the threshold, and she moved back, keeping space between them.

"Evening, darlin'."

"Hello."

"Hope I didn't keep you waiting too long."

"No."

He watched her nervously lick her lips, and closed the distance between them. There was one sure way to knock down the wall of reserve between them. He bent to kiss her, and she let out a sigh of surrender. He deepened the kiss, his tongue sweeping inside her mouth to taste her sweetness as he pulled her closer, molding her luscious curves to his body. His cock sprang into action, swelling as she pressed against him. Groaning, he knew just how needy she felt, as each motion sent a jolt though his cock.

He pulled back before he took her then and there on the doorstep, and really screwed things up. Urging her inside, he shut the door behind him and locked it.

It seemed to break her out of her sensual fever. She stepped back, giving herself breathing room again. He hated it.

"She really was a client. For Pete's sake, Chandra and I went to kindergarten together. She is not now, nor has she ever been, my lover. We used to play at boyfriend/girlfriend, that's all her silly comment meant."

Monica felt her last bit of tension dissolve at the disclosure. She smiled ruefully, taking in his resolute expression. It felt good to have a man she could count on. "I kind of figured that, but it's good to hear you say it. I'm sorry I overreacted."

He shrugged. "I'm not, if it helped settle things between us."

It had, and she was glad of it herself. "Ready to shop?" she asked, stepping up to the counter.

He picked up a hand basket from the stack next to the counter. "Lead me to it."

His enthusiasm bolstered hers. It was time to plan a smashing party. She picked up a few notes she'd made. "I think we should have a theme for the couple's shower, so I came up with a few, but I'd like your opinion."

"What are they?"

She handed him the list. "My top three are Tropic Knights, Evening in Paris, and Fantasy Island."

He grinned. "Definitely Fantasy Island." He smiled at her. "I can think of a few I'd like to try."

"Down, boy," she said, dreaming up a few of her own she'd like to try as she gazed at him amidst her bevy of sexual toys, but that would have to come later. They were still on, her heart was brimming with joy at the realization. Even if it was temporary, it was earthshaking. Not wanting to jinx it, she managed to say calmly, "We can shop for us later."

He went still and raked her with an intense gaze like her capitulation really got to him.

His smile kicked up. "We can?"

She met his gaze with a steady and warm one of her own, and came to a decision. Manhunt or not, it was time to see this this through. "Yes. I've decided to give us a chance and put my manhunt on hold. That is, if you still want to."

"Want to?" He tugged her to him.

She tumbled into his arms, feeling his growing cock hard against her, his heart beating faster as he hugged her. She felt exactly the same way, she decided, melting against him, holding on for the ride.

His hot lips nuzzled her neck as he whispered, "I'm the only man you need, darlin'."

She shivered, wrapping her arms around him. She had to agree. Just as she was heating up, he gently pushed her away, setting her back on her heels.

"Let's get the party shopping out of the way so we can concentrate on us."

Party shopping? How could she concentrate on party shopping when she wanted to tumble him onto the floor and try the Sex Tart's Gel on him?

He picked up a trivia game. "Hey, how about this for starters?"

She sighed, refocusing on the task at hand. "Good choice."

As she followed him down the aisle, her frustrated gaze locked on his tight buns. The man had a killer ass. At that moment, he turned, caught her staring, and grinned. She had the grace to blush. Ogling the man wouldn't get the job done, but damn, it was fun. She glanced from him to the bunnies, remembering when he'd pleasured her with one.

Noting the direction of her stare, he shook his head and smiled. "No bunnies, please."

She grinned back at him, loving the fact that they were so attuned to each other's thoughts. "Right. I don't think all men are as confident as you. They might cause performance anxiety."

She led the way to a worktable in the back of the room and helped him fill gift bags with lubes, lotions, bubble bath, and multicolored party favors. Along with silk leis to bolster the Fantasy Island theme, they'd have the makings of a spicy couple's shower.

"Now it's our turn." He picked up another basket and thrust it at her. "Fill it up, darlin'. Anything you've ever wanted to try."

She couldn't help her face growing hot. She'd never actually shopped for herself with a man at her side. And what a hunky man he was. The smoldering look in his blue eyes gave her confidence.

She walked toward the front of the store, already picturing the lingerie she wanted to buy, but first, the goodies. She picked up Strip Chocolate and saw him smile.

He grinned, and tossed 52 Weeks of Naughty Nights into the basket.

She chuckled, at least she knew what they'd be doing for the next fifty-two days. Or maybe they could accelerate it, and do it twice a day for 26 days. She picked up the Karma Sutra Bedside Box and added it to the basket. Her eyes lingered on Sweet Surrender, and she hesitated. It was a bit kinky. Would he think her a kook for finding it racy? A furtive glance at him told her he noticed the direction of her stare.

Sweat broke out on his forehead as his mouth kicked up in a sexy grin.

He grabbed it and added it to the mix. "This is a big yes."

She smiled, her guard down. "So, you want to tie your cowgirl up, do you?"

"I think I've got just the lasso to do it." He arched a brow, backing her against the counter as he took the basket out of her hand. "And tan your backside, too, if you sass me."

She laughed, getting into the roleplay.

Instead, he stepped away and headed toward the lingerie. He walked past the satin and silk undies, to white lace and soft cotton.

"This, I like." He grabbed the bra and panties, along with stockings and garter belt. A quick look told her he guessed her sizes correctly. The man obviously had a keen eye for figures.

Smiling, she pulled out one of her largest shopping bags. They'd made quite a haul and were going to have some fun.

"Okay, big boy, let's bag this loot up."

"Sure, as soon as you ring it up." He handed her an item.

Even though his tone was light, she recoiled from the words. The idea of him paying her for their pleasure toys didn't sit right with her. It hit a little too close to what some sanctimonious folks called her when she'd decided to go into this business. She made an effort not to freeze, but she knew he noticed her reaction by his frown.

"No, thanks. Consider it market research, and free samples."

He shook his head. "Nothing's free in this life, babe. I pay for what I want."

Surprised by his stubborn reaction, she stood her ground, unwilling to back down. "Well, I'm not for sale."

His whole body tensed at the hasty remark, and she wanted to call it back, but it was too late.

A nerve ticked in his jaw as he resolutely kept piling their purchases on the counter for her to ring up. Placing the Sweet Surrender kit on the counter, he fingered the whip, cutting her a direct gaze. "I really could tan your ass for that."

Her body heated at the flash of fire in his eyes. She could almost feel the leather strands heating her bottom. He was just dominant enough to do it. She hadn't meant to insult him with her refusal, but it seemed she had.

Simmering down, she recognized the concern behind his anger. Was she being just as unreasonable? "I'm sorry, Matt. I guess I'm just a little sensitive on the subject."

He laid the last item on the counter and gave her a curious glance. "Why?"

"Whore was my former husband's favorite nasty name for me."

The shock on Matt's face did a lot to soothe her fears.

He took a step forward. "Oh babe, I'm sorry."

He meant it. She could feel it as he stepped closer. Still, she wasn't quite ready to fall into his arms until he understood.

She inched away while he frowned in reaction. "Don't be. It taught me to stand up for myself."

"Want me to go punch out the bastard?"

The offer actually meant a lot. "That'd be kind of hard to do, seeing as he's in prison."

She couldn't quite meet his gaze as he stared back at her in shock.

Smooth, Monica. That's the way to scare a potential lover off. Just tell him you've got a scamming ex in jail.

She wasn't a criminal, had done nothing wrong, but she still was muddied by the same waters. Not to mention Gary's constant threats and nuisance lawsuits. A mail order course in paralegal, combined with boredom and Gary's crooked personality, meant continued trouble.

"If you want to leave, I'll understand."

He closed the distance between them, his eyes narrowed. "Now, I really ought to paddle your ass. Why would you assume something so idiotic?"

"It's happened before. Having an ex who's a jailbird can cool a girl's social life, in addition to being bad for business." Also, being scammed sucked, but she wasn't going to lay any more of her troubles on Matt's broad shoulders.

"Come here, you." He pulled her into his arms.

She wrapped her arms around him, seeking solace and more. As his mouth brushed across her trembling lips, she let go of the painful memories forever. Matt's passion, his taste as his tongue surged into her mouth, mating with hers, made her weak in the knees.

Leaning into him, she kissed him back, her fingers running though his hair.

He picked her up, still kissing her, and carried her to the chaise lounge in the corner.

She sighed, letting him take control, as he sank onto the chaise with her in his lap. In the shadows, she shivered with delight as he slowly peeled down the zipper of her dress. She shrugged the straps off her shoulders, and it fell.

Now *this* was what she needed—craved.

He cupped her breast through her silk bra. "Perfect," he whispered, bending to kiss her, while his other hand slipped between her legs to stroke her through her panties.

She sighed with pleasure, leaning into his touch as he caressed her until she came, her pussy shuddering with ripples. Lying against him, breathing hard, she slowly drifted back to earth. His cock was rock hard under her bottom, making her a little crazy as she wriggled against him.

Groaning, he continued to gently play with her.

She slipped off his lap, ignoring his growl of disapproval. She was just too damned hungry to wait for him to set the pace. Besides, two could play the teasing game. Her dress fell to the floor as she stood trembling with need in front of him. He sat back in the chaise, raking her with the possessive look of a lover. It only made her tremble more, but she stepped out of the puddle of her dress to seduce him. Funny how after all they'd shared, she could feel shy in her undies, but she did.

He reached out to stroke her bare abdomen. "You're beautiful, darlin'."

She shivered with heat. "You, too."

He laughed with delight at her comment, and she reveled in the sexy sound.

Bidden by the need to turn him on, she reached behind her and unhooked her bra, then slowly let it slip off her body. He growled low in his throat, thrilling her. When he turned her around, his hand ran over her bare ass, work rough and hot. She shivered, moaning in reaction.

He stood, stepping close behind her, the bulge of his crotch pressed tight to her ass as he cupped her breasts with his big hands. She moaned, feeling what he had in store for her. She trembled, leaning into his hot hands, finding it incredibly erotic.

And then, one of his hands drifted up to play with her breasts while the other slipped into her thong and found her clit. Her knees wobbled, and she pressed back against his hard body, moaning.

He slipped her panties off her, then gently lowered them both to the floor on their hands and knees, one hand still cupping her sex.

Moaning, her stiff clit tingling as he stroked it with one finger, his zipper came down. Her sex weeping, sopping wet for him, his hard cock butted against the entry to her pussy and then thrust inside.

She wailed, pushing back to meet his stroke. He set a faster pace, gripping her hips, filling her to the hilt, deeper and harder, until skyrockets were going off behind her closed eyes. Moaning his name, her pussy tightened, as waves of orgasm swept through her. She was pulling him inside her, milking him with her orgasm.

He growled, surging, coming deep inside her.

"You're mine, the past doesn't matter."

CHAPTER 9

Monica placed gift bags on a corner table in Matt's house. It was her first glimpse of his home, and she was impressed. She'd half expected him to live in a rustic log home like Will's. Instead, Matt's place was a modern ranch design set in a forest by the lake, complete with a barn and paddock. It was so him. She itched to explore every inch, but that would have to come later. Right now, they had a couple's shower to host.

She glanced out at him as he lit Tiki torches in the yard surrounding his flagstone terrace, growing flushed with anticipation. It was true. She just couldn't get enough of Matt Shepard. It was as if she was afraid her dream man might vaporize in a puff of smoke if she looked away. She still couldn't quite believe she'd given so much of her heart to him so fast, but it felt right. Her disastrous first marriage was at the root of her fears, and she was determined to move past them. Luckily, Matt was pretty much an open book, and she had nothing to fear on that account.

With the food and drink in readiness, they were seeing to the final details. His parents were coming, which gave her a little pause. Matt's mom was a dear, actually shopping at Spice for lingerie from time to time, and his dad was nice, but how would they feel about her dating their son?

Dating. Heck, she'd all but moved in yesterday, what with Matt surprising her by setting up a workroom for her in his den. When she'd started to object, he'd countered it by saying it was more efficient now that she was designing her men's line around him. She'd been just bemused enough to let herself be sold on that bill of goods. On the plus side, she took it as a sign he wanted to continue their affair. Time would tell what the future would bring, and she'd just have to brazen it out like she did everything else in life.

He came inside and strolled her way, smiling that sultry smile that turned her knees to rubber. Her body responded, growing wet and tingly.

Not now, she told herself, trying to get a grip on her over-stimulated senses.

"Happy darlin'?" he asked, walking up to her.

Nodding, she went into his arms with a happy but needy sigh. "Very. How about you? I was afraid this hen party might be dull for you guys."

He chuckled. "Not with you around."

She gazed around the room, satisfied. The Fantasy Island theme was complete with fresh flower leis for April and Will, Tiki torches, loads of exotic blooms, and frosty tropical drinks Matt had set up outside on the patio bar. She smiled against his shoulder, appreciating his confidence in her.

"Did I tell you I like your house?"

"Do you, now?" He hugged her tighter. "I'm glad to hear you say that, seeing as you're acting as hostess here."

Acting! The word bit at her even though she knew he didn't mean it that way. They were playing house and they both knew it. Matt hadn't even mentioned her manhunt lately, not that she wanted to bring it up. She wanted to extend the fantasy a little bit longer.

As she stood in the shelter of his arms, the doorbell rang. She let out a sigh, bracing for the evening to come.

He let her go. "That must be April and Will."

They walked arm-in-arm to the door, and when he disengaged, she noticed, but didn't say anything. It proved that he was still commitment-phobic.

She opened the door to April and Will. "Aloha," she said, draping a lei around April's neck.

"It's gorgeous," April said, exclaiming over the fresh orchid lei.

"And so are you, babe." Will indulgently beamed at her.

"Thanks, honey." April reached up on tiptoes to kiss him.

Monica and Matt exchanged amused glances. She couldn't help being a wee bit envious of their casual manner. Would she and Matt ever be that free and easy with each other? His brooding made her wonder if he was thinking along the same lines.

"Come on in, you two," she said to break the tension.

April and Will broke their kiss and came in.

"You get lei-ed, too," Matt said, handing Will a matching one.

April giggled, blushing.

Will rolled his eyes before putting on the flower lei. "Leave it to my kid brother to put things in perspective."

April and Monica hugged, while Matt and Will exchanged greetings.

"How's it going?" April whispered.

"Fine." Monica said with a smile. She knew that April had an inkling about their love affair even though she'd denied it at the manhunter's meeting. Frankly, she didn't feel up to discussing it yet. "I'm glad you're here early. The other guests should be here soon."

April looked around the great room and the patio beyond. "Great job, Monica. I love the decor. Everything looks beautiful."

"Hey, how about a little praise for the brute labor?" Matt said with a smile.

"How could I forget my future brother-in-law?" She hugged him. "Thanks."

"Hey, don't put the moves on my girl," Will joked.

"Wouldn't think of it," he said, pulling back. "Besides I've got one of my own." He looped his arm around Monica's waist.

She fell against him, startled. Maybe he wasn't as commitment-phobic as she'd assumed. Now she was the one who felt conspicuously on display. Funny thing was, she didn't mind.

An hour later, Matt was behind the bar he'd set up on the patio, mixing drinks while the guests mingled. From the social chatter, he could tell everyone was having a great time. Monica stood in the midst of it all like a tall, voluptuous traffic cop. She took the role of hostess well. So well, he couldn't picture the place without her.

Will wandered up to the bar. "Hey, bro, need a hand?"

"You could salt the rims of the glasses for the next batch of margaritas."

"Sure thing," Will said, setting to work. "You and Monica seem to be getting serious."

Matt shrugged. He wished. Now, he just had to convince her. "One of us might be more serious than the other," he murmured.

Will stopped salting the glasses and slanted a serious glance his way. "You might want to tread carefully, boy. Monica's been burned before and she's wary."

"Believe me, I know it." What did his brother know that he didn't? "Care to tell me exactly what happened?"

"She had an ex who was a real prick."

"This I already know. Too bad he's where I can't reach him."

Will gave him a grim smile of agreement. "I think you'd have to stand in line. She's been studying martial arts for two years. She'd kick his ass, for sure."

Matt chuckled as he cast a warm look her way. "That, I'd like to see."

"Just be careful. I don't want to see April's best friend hurt."

Matt stiffened, bothered by the comment, even though he knew he had it coming. It was true, he'd been the master of non-commitment. Luckily, Will didn't know more lay behind it.

"I won't. This time, I'm not the gun-shy one."

"Glad to hear it. Fact is, I never thought I'd see the day you were ready to settle down again."

Again. That one word made him tense. He looked Will straight in the eye, and saw an awareness that startled him. He'd thought he'd kept it quiet. Obviously, he'd thought wrong.

"You know."

"About Vegas, yeah."

"How long?"

"Since the beginning. I went looking for you and ran into—"

"Crystal," Matt said, her name a bitter taste in his mouth, but it didn't have the power to cripple him anymore. "Damn the lying bitch. I suppose she wanted to humiliate me."

"I'm here to listen when you want to talk."

"I thought I was in love. She was a showgirl. She told me she was pregnant. I offered to marry her. On what was supposed to be our wedding day, she told me the baby wasn't mine. She was screwing around with my boss at the same time, and she was dumping me for him."

"Damn, that's cold."

"Cold enough to break it off, bro. I demanded a paternity test because I wasn't taking her word for anything. That's when things turned nasty. Fernandez blackballed me with the other construction companies, and turned his high-priced lawyers on me. When that didn't work, he had his boys work me over."

"And the kid?"

"There was no kid. It was just a tool she'd used to play us off one another. I didn't find out until I was getting out of the hospital, and she finally decided to level with me, probably to get rid of me. She had a good laugh telling me what a fool I'd been. So, I dragged my ass back here, tail between my legs."

"Hey, I needed you to help me start Ace Builders." He glanced at Monica and April. "The way I see it, we both won."

"I'm beginning to agree with you. Now, I just have to convince her that I'm a changed man."

Monica handed a gift bag to Matt's mother, Cynthia, as she got ready to leave. "Here's a little thank you for coming, Mrs. Shepard."

"I wouldn't have missed it for the world," she said, looking in the bag and giggling. "I love it," she said, pulling out the red silk lei and draping it around her pink turtleneck sweater. "How do I look?"

Monica smiled at her youthful exuberance. She could see where Matt got his zest for life. "Like a dream. You'll dazzle your hubby."

Cynthia chuckled. "Can I have that in writing?"

Monica smiled. "I don't think you need it."

"True, there's still a fire in the furnace, even though there's snow on the roof."

Monica smiled, glancing at Matt chatting with Will on the patio. They'd been talking for some time, and she couldn't help wondering what they were talking about.

"Speaking of fire, how are things going with Matthew?" Mrs. Shepard asked.

Monica went still, the direct question catching her off guard. "Fine."

She smiled. "He seems to have developed a soft spot for you, my dear, and I couldn't be happier."

Monica flushed, practically glowing under Matt's mom's approval. She hadn't really expected it. "Then you don't mind him associating with me?"

"Mind? Don't be silly. Between you and me, it's high time some woman pulled him out of his rut. I want to see all my children happily settled down."

Monica winced. Even she wasn't expecting forever out of this love affair. She was going to be crushed enough if he left her, without worrying about disappointing Matt's mother, too. "Whoa, slow down, Mrs. Shepard. We're just dating. That's all, for now."

"For now?" Cynthia gave her a steady glance. "You're not stringing him along, are you? I don't think he could take that again."

He couldn't take it again? Just who'd done it before? Which woman had made him so gun shy? Gathering her thoughts, she pinned Matt's mother with a steady gaze. "Again? Who?"

Cynthia hesitated, a troubled look coming to her eyes. "To tell the truth, honey, I don't know. All I know is, when he moved home from Las Vegas, he was a changed man. Only one thing I know can do that to a Shepard male, and that's a woman," she said, taking the wrap from her husband and walking away.

Sighing, Monica spent the rest of the party deep in thought. Could she get him to open up? Should she even try? Was Matt hung up on another woman? Finding out that he'd given his heart to another woman would sting, but she had to know. She set her glass down.

After the last guest left, she started cleaning up, putting empty glasses on a tray. At least the party had been a huge success, even if it'd stirred up some troubled thoughts in her mind. No matter the cost, she had to know Matt's heart, his secrets.

Suddenly, he was at her side, like her thoughts had drawn him to her. She opened her mouth to speak, and he took the tray out of her hands.

"Leave it, darlin'," he said with a sultry smile, "and come with me."

"Okay."

Troubled thoughts submerged when she saw the twinkle in his eye. She let him lead her out to the patio. A warm breeze blew her skirt around her legs.

She took a deep breath of the perfumed night air. It was enough to temporarily quiet her troubled thoughts. He'd spread a blanket out under the star-filled sky. It tugged at her heartstrings when she saw the plump pillows and a champagne bucket with a chilling bottle of bubbly inside. He couldn't love another when he treated her this tenderly.

"How beautiful," she said, casting a soft glance his way. He was watching her in that masterful way that made her cream.

He stalked over to her, making her quiver.

"I agree, darlin'," he murmured against her nape. "How incredibly beautiful you are in the moonlight."

She leaned into him as his hot lips scorched a trail down her neck. She burned for him. "This place is perfect."

"The clovers match your eyes. The moment I laid eyes on you, I wanted to make love to you here."

"Were you that sure of me?" she asked.

"Not sure, but hopeful," he said, pulling her into his arms. "I think moon maids have to go nude," he whispered, unzipping her dress.

A delicious tremor rushed through her, making her heart race as her dress fell.

"I agree," she said, gazing up at him in the moonlight. The look of blatant desire in his eyes took her breath away. "This is so perfect."

"You're the one who's perfect, darlin'." He pulled her to him. "I've been watching you all night, thinking about this moment."

Nothing else mattered to her, either. She went into his arms with a needy moan. The fact she was half-nude while he was dressed didn't phaze her. They kissed, and then his mouth slipped down to nuzzle her earlobe. He nipped it, and she gasped as heat raced through her. Her hands snaked under his jacket. She pulled his shirt up in back, aching to touch his skin.

"Hold on, baby, I'll help you." He leaned back, peeled off his jacket, and undid his bolo tie.

Frustrated by his slow striptease, she grabbed the edges of his shirt and yanked. Buttons popped off, flying through the air, and landing on the grass.

Pushing the shirt off his shoulders, her hands were on him immediately, touching his hair-roughened chest. He groaned and leaned into her caress. His fevered reaction created a frisson of heat deep inside her.

"My turn," he growled, reaching back to unhook her bra, as he yanked her close for a deep kiss.

When he pulled away, her breasts popped free, the night breeze tickling them. Dizzy with desire, she gazed at him, bemused, as he slowly drank in the sight of her. His finger ran across her tender peaks, making her nipples pucker. He ran a tentative finger along the curved slopes of her breasts.

"Oh, please."

"Baby, I will."

She gasped at his hot touch. She was so sensitive, and his large hands were warm and strong as he touched her. Her strawberry pink nipples beaded against his palms, and she moaned. All sensation was centered on the aching peaks. His tender strokes felt so good. Pressing against his roughened fingertips, she whimpered at the electric sensation. Embers of passion built up inside her.

"More."

"Oh, baby, you don't have to ask." he said, picking her up to lay her on the blanket. He bent to take her nipple into his hot mouth, slowly sucking on it.

She groaned, feeling a tug deep inside. She held him close as he moved from one to the other, sucking hard, sending pleasure rocking through her. Out of her head with pleasure, as he suckled, teasing first one and then the other peak, she scraped her nails along his back, writhing on the blanket.

He groaned, pulling down her panties until she was nude. She let out a gasp when his big hand cupped her mound. She whimpered, pressing against his warm palm. She ached—she needed. Her legs thrashed on the blanket. She arched, reveling in his fiery touch. She could feel herself growing wet and ready for him.

Throwing one of his heavy legs over hers to hold her still, he pressed her into the blanket. His cock was hard against her thigh, and she wanted it so badly. And he obviously wanted her just as bad as she wanted him. Trembling, she burned with a hunger for him. Running her hand over his rock hard erection, she felt the heat and length of him. She fumbled with his zipper.

His fingers went right to her clit, rubbing it, pinching it, until her legs spread wide. She lifted herself off the blanket, whimpering for more.

"That's right, darlin'. Go wild for me." He slipped one, then two fingers, into her wet heat.

She started to come, her spasms tugging his fingers deep inside. A fierce orgasm tore through her, tightening all her muscles.

He eased her back and knelt between her spread legs, his cock butting against her quivering pussy, and then surged into her.

She cried out, clinging to him, her hips snapping up to match his thrusts. Her body shook, contractions drawing him deeper as she came, shouting his name.

He came, then rolled over to have her sprawl on top of him.

She reveled in his closeness. She slowly drifted back to earth, feeling closer to him than ever before.

"Matthew, let's talk."

"About what?"

"Us, for starters. You know so much about me, but I know very little about you."

"You know all that's important."

"Do I?" She felt him turn stiff, and knew she'd run up against a brick wall. She had to know what stood between them, or at least, show him she was there if he wanted to talk. "Matt, I—"

"There's something I should tell you."

She sighed and snuggled closer, even though she felt him tense. Was this where he let her down easy?

"Who is she?" she asked.

"She?"

"The girl you're hung up on."

He pulled back to look at her curiously. "That'd be you."

"Me? But..." She was so startled, she didn't know quite what to say. "But then, who've you been carrying a torch for?"

"There was someone once, but that was over long ago."

"Oh." She calmed down, deciding to give him the benefit of the doubt. He was obviously tense about this. "Go on."

"I almost got married, but it didn't work out."

"Why?"

"Let's just say I found out she was playing me for a sucker. I won't make the same mistake twice."

That explained his love 'em and leave 'em MO. But where did it leave her?

"I see," she said, not seeing at all. Would he ever be ready to take a chance on love?

Three days later, Matt stood satisfied as he surveyed the motley crew of male models he'd assembled in Spice's backroom. He'd come through, and he felt like a hero when Monica had gazed at him in gratitude. It was worth the struggle. He'd begged, borrowed, and called in some favors to get a few other male models for this demo for Monica's sales clerks and distributors.

"You owe me big time for this bro," Will said, cinching the robe tight around his middle to cover up the white boxers covered with red hearts.

"What are you complaining about? I'm the one stuck wearing these babies," Matt said, indicating his red silk boxers. They sure as hell didn't hide what he was packing. "Besides, she's giving you the whole collection for your trousseau."

Will frowned. "Yeah, what the hell is a trousseau anyway?"

"Damned if I know," Dwain said, stalking out of the dressing room in plaid boxers and a sleeveless t-shirt.

"Hey, guys, how's it going?" Monica said, poking her head in the door.

"Do you mind? We're still dressing," hollered Andy.

"You mean undressing," Dwain muttered, shooting Matt a dark look.

"Calm down, guys. You all look great, and it's nothing you don't already show on the beach," she said with a grin. "I'll be waiting up front. Come out when you're ready."

CHAPTER 10

Half an hour into Will's bachelor party, Matt sidled up to him at the bar in Red's party room, trying to tune out the blare of the stripper Tiffany's boom box. He grabbed a ginger ale and glanced at his watch, counting the minutes until he could sneak out the back door and get back to Monica.

They'd been all but inseparable since the couple's shower two nights before, and he meant to keep it that way. He'd even taken the liberty of bringing over her design supplies. She'd been bemused, only voicing a small objection, which he'd countered by pointing out it was more efficient, seeing as he was acting as model for her men's line of underwear. He'd done it to keep her close, but he'd found himself delighted by being on the inside of her design process, not to mention, being measured every which way could be good for a guy's ego. He chuckled, remembering her comments and his payback when they played Sweet Surrender later in the bedroom. They'd both taken to the role-play BD game.

"Hey, bro," Will said in greeting, giving the stripper an absentminded glance.

Matt scanned the stag-line with front row seats around the small stage. Most of the guys had stupid grins on their faces and fistfuls of ones for her g-string, telling him the party was a big success, even if it didn't feel that way to him. Dwain, he noticed, hung back from the crowd, although he watched the stripper with interest.

Matt's disinterested gaze flicked over Tiffany for a second as he recalled Monica teasing him about hiring a stripper. The dancer's charms, while bountiful, couldn't hold a candle to what was waiting for him at home. Hell, truth to be told, he couldn't even spend much time away from Monica without going though withdrawal pangs. It was a worrisome thing to need a woman this bad, but his love was worth the risk.

Trying to get with the swing of the evening, Matt pasted a smile on his face and found Will watching him with a doubtful look.

"Having fun yet?" Matt shouted to be heard over the raucous chatter from the other guys.

"Sure am." Will smiled, and hoisted his longneck bottle of beer.

Matt leaned back against the bar and looked at him unconvinced. Will looked just as bored. "Oh yeah? Then why aren't you down front stuffing dollar bills down Tiffany's G-string?"

Will caught Tiffany's bra when she lobbed it their way, laid it on the bar, and turned to Matt. "First thing a soon to be married man should know, if you've got something sweeter at home, don't fuck it up."

"Damn, you're getting old," Matt teased, but he understood completely. His heart and mind weren't here, either.

"Mature, yeah." He agreed with a negligent shrug. "And you ain't fooling me none, kid. You've been edging toward the door since we got here." Will set down his beer and looked at him. "Do you want to bail?"

Matt nodded ruefully. "Yeah. I didn't know I was that easy to read. Monica's home, waiting for me."

"So go, boy, don't fuck it up."

That was the plan, not doing anything to screw it up.

A feeling of relief settled over him. Another hurdle crossed. Still, there was a part of him that worried it could all blow up in his face. Having Monica move in with him temporarily was a heavenly fluke, but was it coming too easy? It seemed like they'd never stopped having fun exploring their love toys. Now, the only problem was talking her into making things more permanent, her manhunt list be damned.

"You don't mind?"

"Hell no, of course, I don't mind. You've found someone worth going home for, and you're in love."

Hearing the L word said out loud was a hurdle he hadn't even crossed himself yet, but it was true. It was love, not just lust. It was raw, new, but real. Still, acknowledging it didn't do him any good. Monica was so skittish, still needing to feel in control, he couldn't help wondering why she didn't trust him enough to let go.

"We haven't quite gotten that far, bro."

"You will."

"I guess I'll get going then." He looked at the guys down front, enjoying the show. "Think they'll miss me?"

"Doubt it," Will said with a smile as he watched dollar bills being thrust in the stripper's G-string. "I don't even think they'll miss me when I leave in about half an hour."

"Sorry the bachelor party was such a bust."

"Nah, it was perfect. I just think we've outgrown this kid's stuff."

"Damn. Maturity, it's a sobering thought." It was true. He'd rather have a romantic time with Monica than a hot time on the town. "I'm out."

Matt left Red's back party room to pass through the bar to the tune of Will's laughter. One minute he was weaving his way through the Saturday night crowd, and the next, a drunk blundered into his path.

Matt drew to a halt, the background noise fading as he took in the scowling man's belligerent stance. Half a head shorter, with mean eyes and drunk off his ass, the guy was obviously spoiling for a fight.

Frowning back at the man, as the stink of stale beer wafted across the three feet that separated them, Matt let out a world-weary sigh. Damn, he didn't need this. He had a woman to get home to.

"You don't want any part of this, buddy," he said, moving to step around him.

The drunk staggered to maintain his blockade, grumbling, "Hell no, you ain't walking away from me, Shepard. You'll back off my woman, asshole, if you know what's good for you."

Matt froze, staring at the drunk's ruddy face as he tried unsuccessfully to place the man, mentally running through the guys on Monica's manhunt list. "Your woman?" he asked softly, not liking the fact that half the bar suddenly seemed to be listening in. He didn't want Monica's name dragged through the mud.

"You heard me, dumb ass," the drunk said, puffing his chest out. "Don't deny it. My buddy told me what you two've been doing behind my back."

His buddy? Glancing toward the bar, Matt spotted Ted Miller standing there, watching them avidly, and figured it out. Too much of a coward to fight his own battles, it seemed Miller was trying to get even by stirring up trouble. Although, how he knew about the list, Matt didn't know. As far as he knew, he was the only man privy to that information. Right now, the whys and hows didn't matter, he was too pissed off to care.

"Damn, I should have clobbered the prick," he muttered, shouldering the drunken man aside to get to the real instigator.

"Hey, where do you think you're going?" the drunk howled.

Matt ignored him, homing in on his target. He first saw awareness, and then fear in Miller's eyes as he backed away, bumping up against the bar.

Suddenly, Miller's gaze shifted to something behind him.

Matt had an inkling of disaster an instant before a pool cue hit him. He ducked and it grazed a glancing blow, making him see stars, before crashing on his shoulder and against the bar.

Amidst the tinkle of smashing glass, screams and shouts, Matt spun around and used the drunk's momentum to throw him across the room. He crashed into the wall and slid down it, unconscious. With a growl, Matt turned to take care of Miller as Dwain and Will, followed by the rest of the bachelor party, came tearing out of the back room.

"I didn't do nothing," Miller wailed, slinking through the crowd toward the door.

Taking in the situation in a glance, Dwain grabbed Miller before Matt could get to him. "You're not going anywhere until I sort this out."

"I didn't do anything," he grumbled, flashing a glare at Matt. "He's the one that started this brawl."

The drunk moaned and rolled over, starting to come to.

Dwain looked down at him and froze. "Damn, when'd they let him out?" He pulled out his cell phone. "Yeah, send a black and white to Red's. I've got two for pick-up. I suspect one's a parole violator."

Parole violator! Matt put it all together in an instant, despite his rattled brain. This had to be Monica's jailbird ex-husband lying in a stinking heap on the floor. A cool rage settled in his body as he took a step toward the man to rip him apart.

"Don't," Dwain said, stepping between them. "He's not worth it."

Matt stopped, glaring at Dwain for a moment before sanity returned. It didn't help he still wanted to break the guy. He knew this wasn't over by a long shot. The guy would be trouble if allowed to run free.

"I want him gone."

"He will be," Dwain hurried to reassure him. "Don't worry. The courts take a dim view of parole violators who start bar fights." Dwain nodded to Will. "You want to take care of your brother, and make sure he stays out of trouble?"

"Sure." Will pushed Matt toward the bar. "Come on, let's get you patched up."

"Patched up?"

A warm trickle fell from his scalp as Will urged him onto an empty bar stool. Red handed Will a clean bar towel, but Matt only had eyes for Gary as he was arrested. What was Monica holding back from him? She still had secrets, he could feel it.

"What'd he do to wind up in prison?" Matt asked with a pained grimace as Will pressed the bar towel to the cut on the back of his head.

"She didn't tell you?"

"No." He waited while Will seemingly considered things.

"If you can believe it, he was a one-time successful investment banker. Turned out, he was a crook. He took a lot of people in the area down, including Monica. When she found out about it, she turned him in, and that's when he turned nasty. The cops had to haul him off of her. But that girl is a fighter. She came out of it stronger than ever. On top of that, she pulled herself out of debt and made restitution to his victims, even though she went through far worse. The guy's been a pain in the ass for the three years he's been incarcerated, threatening her from prison. I can't believe they let him out. You'd better make sure she's safe."

A chill went through Matt when he considered what a close call she'd had. He closed his eyes and thanked whatever wild angel had kept her at his place and out of danger.

"She's at my house."

"Good, see that she stays there."

"Don't worry, I intend to," Matt said, wincing. His head and shoulder were throbbing in tandem, but the pain helped him focus.

Dwain walked over to them, his concerned gaze flickering over Matt. "He need medical attention?"

"Nah, I'm good," Matt protested. "Will rendered some first aid. Well, what did you find out?"

Dwain scowled. "It ain't good. They let him out early for good behavior, which means he *is* on parole, like I figured. If you agree to press charges, we can put him back in prison for the remainder of his sentence."

"Hell yeah, I'll press charges," Matt vowed. "As far as I'm concerned, they can throw away the key. The bastard's lucky you stepped in when you did."

"I'll do my damnedest to make sure we keep him locked up until his parole hearing. Funny, they didn't notify Monica of his release."

Matt felt a little twinge of guilt. He'd monopolized her time, and for selfish reasons. He didn't want her to go back to her manhunt, and keeping her busy loving him seemed like a good way to achieve his goal.

"She hasn't been home. She's been staying at my place."

"That explains it, then. You want me to break the news?"

"No, I'll do it." Matt got to his feet. "I think it'll be better coming from me."

CHAPTER 11

Monica put French roast coffee on to brew, and turned to get the last tray of chocolate chunk cookies out of the oven. She was going to surprise Matt with her domestic qualities. The mingled aromas smelled heavenly as she tidied up. Matt had said he'd try to get away early, and she intended to surprise him with a little game of Sweet Surrender. Her bottom heated at the thought as her libido simmered. Playing with Matt had brought out the wild and kinky side of her she'd kept under wraps.

She heard the door open, and Matt's footsteps cross the tile floor of the foyer. When he walked into the kitchen, she flung herself at him with a smile.

"Welcome home, honey."

"You didn't lock the door."

His gruff tone, accompanied by his stiff body, set off warning bells inside her. Something was wrong. Maybe he'd gotten a taste of the wild life at the bachelor party and was regretting their affair?

Even as she thought it, she rejected it. He was in it for the long haul just like she was. "Sorry, I guess I forgot. I knew you were coming home." She gave him a peck on the cheek and was rewarded with a bear hug. Gasping for breath, she managed to ask, "What's wrong, Matthew?"

Wincing, he let her go. "I got in a little bar fight."

She pulled away far enough to take in the bandage on the back of Matt's head and his troubled expression. "Are you okay?"

"I'm fine."

She didn't believe that for one second. "Well, it must have been one hell of a fight then, because you look like someone just stole your favorite toy."

His wince made her worry even more. Could he be hurt worse than she thought?

"I'm fine. Red gave me a bar towel and a band-aid."

That thought made her cringe. Red wasn't known for his cleanliness.

She tugged him over to the dinette. "Great, you'll probably get ptomaine. Sit." She shoved him down into a chair, and he toppled with an indulgent smile that made her knees wobble.

"I'm okay, babe."

"I'll be the judge of that." She peeled off the blood-soaked bandage to see a bloody slice across the back of his head. "Did some guy cut you?"

"No. A drunk took a pool cue to my head."

That word picture was enough to make her shudder. "And what does he look like?"

"Not a scratch on him. He's cooling his heels in jail."

"My hero," she said, beaming at him. It only meant to prove his power, impressing the hell out of her. "It's just like the other night with number six," she said proudly, getting the first aid kit from under the sink.

"He was there," Matt said casually.

Just like Ted's groping of her a few weeks back. He'd come at her from behind. What a coward. "He hit you?"

"Nah, he just instigated it. He's too chicken to fight his own battles."

That was true, but what was Matt holding back? If Ted instigated it, that meant it was over her. The thought saddened her. She certainly never intended to be the cause of trouble. She cleaned the wound with antiseptic, and winced in sympathy as Matt stiffened. It wasn't deep, but it was still oozing blood.

"I think maybe you need stitches."

"No, thanks. I'll be okay."

Knowing he'd keep refusing despite her concerns, she applied gentle pressure to the wound for a few moments, and the bleeding stilled. Reading between the lines, she knew that the fight had been about her. Matt, her hero, had defended her honor. It touched her even though she hated the thought of him getting hurt.

She put the bandage on. "All done."

"Thanks," he said. "We need to talk."

His tone worried her. "What's wrong?"

"Your ex is out of prison."

Gary? Why hadn't she been informed? Warned?

She stood frozen as the enormity of the bombshell sunk in. He'd been the drunk with the pool cue who'd attacked Matt. She didn't need to be told. She really *was* the cause of Matt's pain, and not in an indirect way. The sneak attack fit Gary's MO to a T. He'd tried to strangle her when she'd turned him in for theft. She'd tried to relegate him to ancient history, but he was pushing himself back into her life like a poison, killing everything he touched.

Looking at Matt's injuries, her heart sank. "He attacked you."

"From behind, yeah. He's back in jail now. I'm pressing charges, so Dwain says he's sure to serve the remainder of his sentence and—"

"He won't like that." Monica relived the nightmare of being throttled as Matt looked back at her with a worried expression. Gary, she could handle. Hell, she'd studied martial arts just so she could kick his ass if he ever resurfaced to get even with her, but she couldn't have him lying in wait for Matt.

"Are you okay?"

She took a deep breath and tried not to cry as her dreams for the future went up in smoke. "I don't think so. I'm so sorry I got you into this. I'll pack my bags and—"

"Like hell." Matt pulled her stiff body onto his lap.

She tried to stand, but his arm around her waist wouldn't let her. "I've got to. You won't be safe."

"No." He stood, picking her up, and cradling her to him. "He's in jail and he can't touch us."

She wasn't so sure. She'd thought he'd been safely put away, and he wasn't. Still, as Matt's soothing caress turned sensual, she let herself be lured into a sense of security.

"Remember your code word."

Her whole body heated, melting into him as he carried her. The crisis settled into the background as physical sensation came into play. She was so attuned to Matt's magic touch, the code word from their game, and she was about to get a sexy spanking. She'd already had three, and he knew how hot it made her. All she had to do was say 'strawberry,' and he'd stop. Held tight, listening to the reassuring thud of his heartbeat, she didn't want to. The man was a dirty fighter, using her sexual wants against her.

She sighed, pressing a soft kiss to his tight jaw, and felt it relax, slowly gaining strength from him. He really was too good to be true. Her homicidal ex had attacked him, and he was still standing strong. Could she do any less for him?

When he carried her to the bedroom, she didn't resist. Couldn't have, even if she wanted to. She wanted this, needed him.

"Time to play," he said, setting her on her feet, and peeling off her clothes while bending to kiss her.

She moaned as his mouth claimed hers, his tongue thrusting into her mouth. She pressed against him, on fire as the Velcro cuff wrapped around her left wrist. Her pulse and libido did a leap.

Breaking the kiss, he bent to nibble on her nape. "It's time for you to surrender to your man."

A little fission of excitement and alarm zinged through her. It was always like this. "So, I'm your prisoner?" she murmured, as he cuffed her other wrist and bent her over the settee.

"I think that might be the other way around," he said, reaching for the soft cloth whip.

She let out a hiss of excitement as the whip came down on her bottom. There was more heat than pain, and she was instantly aroused. Biting back a moan and trembling as he played the whip up and down her hot bottom, she got wet with desire, her pussy quivering.

"Oh." She arched her hips leaning into the strokes.

"I'm not some idiot you can push away to keep me safe. Don't you forget it again," he said with a final slap of the whip.

"Yes, Sundance," she said, meaning it.

She wouldn't let Gary's specter haunt her anymore. He was the past, and Matt was her future. When he dropped the whip and lifted her up, she fell into his arms, overwhelmed with hunger for his touch. She kissed him as he carried her to bed. Tumbling down onto it, her hot bottom hit the cool sheets and she moaned.

He nibbled her ear. "God, you're sexy, woman, and you're driving me crazy."

She laughed, amused and bedazzled. "I think I've cornered the market on crazy. Who just got spanked?"

He stilled for a moment, pulling away to look at her. "I didn't hurt you, did I?"

"No." She insisted, tugging him down again. "I don't think that soft whip could actually hurt anyone."

He growled, rolling her over. "I'll have to pick up a paddle for next time."

She laughed at the threat. "I'd probably let you. But first..."

"You need something from me," he teased, his gaze locked with hers as his stiff cock pressed against the slick entrance of her pussy.

Monica fell into the blue depths of his eyes and couldn't look away while his cock teased her tantalizingly within reach, but not taking her.

"Ah, yes. Fill me, Sundance," she said with a needy sigh as the broad head of his cock eased inside her trembling pussy.

She cried out, clinging to him as he slid home. He held still for a moment, throbbing inside her as he bent to kiss her. Wrapping herself around him, she shuddered when he started to move, faster and deeper. Her pussy rippled with waves of ecstasy.

"Come for me," he demanded, deepening the thrusts.

And she did, climaxing, her spasms clamping onto him as he came deep inside her.

CHAPTER 12

Monica walked back into the party room at Finnegan's Supper Club, which she'd booked for April's shower, dejected, after learning her entertainment had cancelled. Twenty minutes before the shower, she'd called the male revue to see why they were late, only to find out that they'd double-booked and weren't coming. What in the heck was she going to do with twenty guests and no entertainment? It was going to be a pretty ho hum bachelorette party, and she wanted so much for this to be special for April.

Coming on top of last night's fiasco, it seemed like the fates were lined up against her. What else could go wrong? Who'd believe that a flawed prison system would let Gary out early, or that he'd get drunk and go after Matt? Now this was too much.

Courtney and Toni looked up from the decorations they were putting up, and headed her way.

"What's the verdict?" Courtney asked.

"They're not coming." She recalled her heated argument with the male revue's booking agent.

"What do you mean, they're not coming?" Toni frowned. "It's breach of contract. I'll sue them."

"Like that's going to do us a fat lot of good now," Monica said with a shake of her head. Seeing Toni's distress, she softened her tone. "For a hard-nosed cop, you can be awfully naive, girlfriend. Apparently, they got a better offer."

"Oh, damn," Emily said. "What are we going to do? We've got a dozen wild women arriving in half an hour for the bachelorette party and no entertainment."

They all grinned because Emily never swore.

"That's salty talk coming from you." Courtney said.

Toni sighed. "Anybody know a good male revue we can get at the last minute?"

Monica and Courtney looked at each other and smiled.

"Actually, I think maybe we do, but it's a long shot."

"Well, go get them girl."

Monica whipped out her phone and made her way to a quiet corner for privacy. How to talk her unsuspecting lover and his pals into stripping?

Half an hour later, she handed her male line of garments through the men's room door to her reluctant models. "You don't have to strip, guys. I'll just turn the music on, and you can strut your stuff."

"I don't know about this," Will grumbled.

She tensed. "Guys, I owe you big time for doing this. Just remember, you're doing this for April."

Peering through the crack, she saw a few of them nodding and stripping. Closing her eyes, she pressed back against the wall, adding as a last incentive, "Look at the bright side, Will. Your bride-to-be won't be ogling a male stripper."

"Sounds like a good reason to me," Will said. "All right, guys, get 'em off for my lady."

Fanning her flushed face, Monica made her way back to the party room and homed in on April, who sat smiling, surrounded by her opened gifts.

"You've all been far too generous." April smiled. Looking at Monica, she picked up her hot pink bunny. "Especially you."

Everyone laughed.

"You haven't seen anything yet, girlfriend," Monica said with a grin. "Wait until you see the special entertainment we've arranged." She pushed the button on the boombox, sitting on the edge of the stage. "And now, for your pleasure, I present the groomsmen, plus one."

"Oh no," April said with a blush and laugh.

Monica sat next to April just as Matt walked out of the wings to hoots and whistles.

"Yum," Toni yelled.

Monica couldn't agree more. Matt looked like heaven in his red satin boxers. "Here is Matt in midnight rendezvous."

The ladies applauded.

He winked and stuck a pose.

Andy Wallace came strutting out in blue briefs.

"And next is Andrew in electric blue."

He did a few dance moves and hurried off the stage.

When he walked off, Dwain, who stood on the edge, was pushed onto stage. He turned to scowl at the guys behind him, but the applause made him face the ladies. A flush stained his cheeks. Tall, with sandy hair, he had a powerful build.

Monica stifled a laugh. "Next is Dwain, modeling happy holidays, a tank top worn with plaid boxers for fun."

Dwain cracked a little smile and did a turn on the stage, his gaze scanning the crowd before stopping on Toni, who giggled and looked away.

"And last but not least, Will in honeymoon hello."

Will strutted out in a short white robe over white briefs.

April laughed. "At least you didn't put him in a thong."

He chuckled and lifted up his robe to reveal two bare buns.

"Oh Lord, you didn't." April laughed.

"I always save the best for last," Monica said with a smile.

CHAPTER 13

Monica made her way back home from the bachelorette party, pleased. It had all gone well, and she owed Matt and her models big time. Too bad they hadn't stuck around. Still, she could understand their reasons. They weren't used to being seen as sex objects.

She'd just have to make it up to Matt in bed, she thought with a wicked chuckle. She was going to show him just how devoted she was. Unfortunately, his pickup wasn't in the driveway, which meant she beat him home. Still, it would give her time to prepare. Handcuffs, whipped cream, and her paddle would make for a hot evening.

She got out of the car and let herself in to set things up. *Letting herself in with his key.* She thought about how far they'd come. They were living together. Unofficially, of course, but that didn't make it any less true. She went into the kitchen and plopped her tote bag down.

A glance at the reflective glass of the patio door showed a dark moving shape behind her. Her heart pounded.

She feinted to the side, spinning around just as a wine bottle swung at her head. It smashed against the cabinet, spewing red wine. Her blood ran cold when she got a look at Gary's enraged face. He was meaner and heavier, but there was no mistaking him. How had he gotten out of jail? Again.

"Damn you and your boyfriend, bitch. Tell him to drop the charges, or else."

"Are you crazy? You belong in a mental ward," she hissed, going fluid as her sensei had taught her. She'd studied for just this occasion, and brains could beat brawn.

He started toward her. "And you belong in the ground. Guess which one of us is gonna get their wish if you don't do as I say."

"He's not here." She backed away into the open area of the great room, and he followed her. Matt would be home soon, she just needed to keep stalling, and she wouldn't be alone with Gary for long. "Leave now, and I won't turn you in."

He laughed. "Yeah, right," he bit out, lunging toward her.

She sprang forward, grabbed his wrist, and flung him over her hip. He crashed against the coffee table, cracking his head, and flopping on the ground. She jammed her stiletto in his groin just as the front door burst open.

Matt came rushing in, followed by the police.

He took one look at her, and pulled her into his arms. "Oh, babe, are you okay?"

She sagged against him. "I am now."

Dwain cuffed Gary and handed him over to the police. "Get this scum out of here."

Matt held Monica in his lap after Dwain left, scared. He'd almost lost the love of his life! Stunned, he couldn't handle it.

For her part, she'd gone silent, just leaning against him as if for strength.

"I didn't know he was here. I didn't see him, except at the last minute."

"I know, babe, I'm sorry. Dwain told me he was let go on a technicality, and we came as quick as we could. I wasn't there for you."

"I handled him."

"Yes, you did," he said, feeling a sense of pride. "You were magnificent."

She looked at the shattered bottle and spilled wine. "He made a mess of your floor. I should..."

"I'll clean it up. I think you need some care."

He picked her up and carried her through the bedroom, and into the master bath. He filled the Jacuzzi and added the jasmine bath oil she liked, then he tenderly undressed her and lowered them both into the tub.

She sighed, leaning back against him. He cradled her in the shelter of his arms, kissing the top of her head.

"You are good for what ails me, Sundance."

"Happy to oblige," he said, his cock throbbing as it grew against her soft bottom. He grabbed a sea sponge and washed her front, paying particular attention to her breasts. Her nipples budded, and she moaned as he scrubbed them.

Monica loved the feel of Matt's wet slick body against hers. When he turned her in the tub, she let out a needy moan. He slanted a kiss across her lips. She straddled him, her mouth opening under his as his big hands sought her breasts under the water, cupping them. She arched, begging for his sweet attention.

He pinched the nipples, and she whimpered into his mouth. They budded, aching for him, and he bent to take one in his mouth. She rubbed her pussy against his hard cock, gasping at the pleasure the small movement brought. She reached for his hard cock, capturing him in a confident grip.

He growled, thrusting himself into her hands. His drifted from her breast to tease her pussy, and she was lost in sensation. He pressed against her clit, and she moaned, gripping him even tighter. She quivered as he slid one, then two fingers into her, teasing her, testing her readiness. His digits moved in and out of her faster, as she clenched around him, and then he withdrew.

He picked her up, lifting her high so her breasts dangled like ripe fruit, suckling one and then the other nipple until they were wet and hard. He drew hungrily at the sweet, strawberry peaked globes. Squirming against him, as she hovered over him, brushing tantalizingly against his manhood, she cried out.

He slowly lowered her onto his cock, slipping deep inside her quivering pussy. She ground against him, moaning, but he held her hips, restraining her movements. She stilled for a second, but her internal ripples tugged at him.

He bent to nibble her ear while one hand pinched her nipple, and she exploded, coming.

When it was all over, he was still rock hard inside her. "What are you waiting for, Matt, an engraved invitation?" She nipped at his shoulder, wriggling against him.

"Be patient." He spanked her ass under water.

She pouted, stung but amused, despite herself. So, he wanted to draw it out, did he?

Cupping her ass, he started to move, and she gasped as her fiery passion returned double-fold. He set a slow, deliberate pace that gradually grew faster and faster. She clung to him, arching to meet his thrusts as he wrung another orgasm out of her. Sucking on his neck, she shrieked out his name as she came, her spasms tugging him.

He came, pounding into her two more times, holding her to him as he buried himself to the hilt.

He sagged against him, comforted as he held her tightly.

CHAPTER 14

Matt stood beside Will at the altar as the wedding march started to play. A quick glance at his brother told him he was holding up pretty well despite the stiff set of Will's shoulders in the tux he was wearing.

As Toni, the first bridesmaid, started down the aisle in a long lilac gown, Matt surreptitiously patted his pocket to make sure he still had the ring.

He still felt kind of raw after Monica's close call last night, and he didn't want his distracted thinking to affect his brother's wedding. A glance at Dwain, who was standing as a groomsman on his other side, told him the guy was watching him warily. He didn't approve of their plan to keep the attack quiet until after the wedding, but Monica had been adamant, and Matt was in the mood to indulge her. The guy was back behind bars, so why did he still feel like wrapping her in cotton wool and tucking her away where nobody could touch her?

Because their idyll was coming to an end. She'd agreed to table her manhunt until after the wedding, and his time to win her was almost up.

The moment Monica came down the aisle, Matt's breath caught in his throat. She was so beautiful. Her gaze passed warmly over Will to lock firmly with Matt's. He felt a little surge of heat and pride. He loved her.

At the end of the ceremony, he linked arms with Monica. The time had come to tell her how he felt. He only hoped she reciprocated.

At the reception, Monica joined Courtney, Toni, and the pack at a table in the ballroom.

"Manhunters unite! One down and only four more to go," Toni joked.

Monica rolled her tired feet and glanced across the room at Matt and Dwain talking. "Count me out."

Courtney let out an excited gasp. "Don't tell me my brother's proposed."

"No, he hasn't," Monica cut in, feeling a little pang. "We're simply dating." He didn't want marriage, which he'd said from the start.

"How about me," Emily piped in. "Anybody know any hot prospects?"

"How about Ted Miller," Jo asked.

"Oh no, not him," the others chimed in unison.

"Why not?" she asked.

"Believe me, he's bad news," Monica said. "The man's all hands, besides being a drunk and a coward."

Jo winced. "Thanks for warning me."

"It's the least one manhunter can do for another," Monica said, and noticed Matt's approach.

She wanted to dance with her man while she still had him. After the wedding, would she be like Cinderella turning back into a dateless pumpkin? He hadn't asked for more.

As they waltzed across the floor, she noticed he held her a little tighter than usual, and didn't mind a bit. She leaned into his strength, loving the way his body felt pressed tight against hers.

The next morning, Monica woke up alone. She reached for Matt's pillow to find it cold and empty.

Was he back to business as usual so quick? It was a demoralizing thought. Then again, maybe he was making her breakfast. Keeping that positive thought, she slipped on her robe and padded toward the kitchen.

She glanced around the kitchen, finding it empty, and her heart sank. A sound made her turn toward the great room.

Matt was there, sitting on the floor with a wrapped gift. "Come here," he said, crooking his finger.

She walked to him, drawn like a moth to a flame. He was still here. She sank on the floor next to him and took the beautifully wrapped gift he handed her.

"For me?"

"Who else?"

"What's the occasion?"

"It's a love gift. Open it and find out."

Love gift? Was he saying what she thought he was saying?

Tearing off the gold paper, she found a box. Opening the box, she found her planner lying in pink tissue paper.

"My planner," she said, surprised, and a bit let down. She'd half expected hearts and flowers, a million candy hearts, something romantic.

"Open it."

She lifted it, noticing it felt a tiny bit different. She opened the cover, finding it stiffer. There on the first page was Matt's name written in red ink about a million times. He must have been up half the night writing it. Did it mean what she thought it did?

She looked up at him in wonder. He was smiling, but there was a hint of nervousness in his eyes. How endearing.

He pulled out a jeweler's box from his pocket, and flipped it open.

She looked at the beautiful solitaire engagement ring, the diamond flanked by emeralds the color of her eyes, and got teary. She smiled at him through her tears, memorizing the picture of the hunk she loved, offering his heart.

He leaned in to brush a tear off her cheek. "I propose that you take on a manhunt of one, darlin'."

She leaned forward to kiss him. "Yes! I think I just bagged my limit."

He laughed, and they made love amidst the tissue paper.

CHECK OUT MORE ROMANCES FROM ROWAN PROSE PUBLISHING!

Julie Castle is a natural-born romantic with a modicum of artistic talent inherited from her mom and a love for telling tall tales she got from her dad. That set her up for being a starving artist, the biggest fibber in the world, or a romance author. She's so glad she chose the latter. She's always had a love affair with the written word. As a child growing up in a small town, she loved visiting the local library, a converted gilded age mansion, and getting lost between the pages of a book. The drafty old mansion could be a spooky place, but she still loved it. She enjoyed poking into behind the scenes areas she wasn't supposed to venture into. She's still the same way, which is why she loves writing romance with an edge, paranormal, suspenseful, super sexy, or just laugh your pants off funny. She resides in Wisconsin with her family.